COVEN

Thomas Brown

Lynnwood

Sparkling Books

British Library Cataloguing in Publication Data. A catalogue record for this book is available from the British Library.

2.1

BIC code: FK
ISBN: 978-1-907230-38-7

Printed in the United Kingdom by Berforts Information Press

@SparklingBooks

Praise for *Lynnwood*

'*I would recommend this to fans of classic English horror as well as fans of Stephen King.*'
Lucy O'Connor, Waterstones bookseller

"*A quintessentially British folk horror chiller, with an escalating power of dread that is rendered deftly. A new voice in British horror, that you'll want to read, has entered the field.*"
Adam Nevill, Author of *Apartment 16* and *The Ritual*

'*The plot line is new and exciting, I won't say anymore about that because I don't want to give it away! But I know I was surprised more than once at what was happening. If you are looking for a good book, definitely pick up this one.*'
Alison Mudge, Librarian, USA

'*An exciting, on the edge of your seat gothic that will have readers begging for more.*'
Rosemary Smith, Librarian and Cayocosta Book Reviews

'*An exciting début from a new young writer with a dark imagination. Thomas Brown's beautifully written novel proposes a modern gothic forest far from the tourist trail, a place filled with strange events and eerie consequences.*'
Philip Hoare 'one of the world's most famous and celebrated chroniclers of the New Forest and its history'

Thomas Brown is a postgraduate student at the University of Southampton, where he is studying for an MA in Creative Writing.

He has been Co-Editor of Dark River Press and has written for a number of magazines, websites and independent publishers.

In 2010 he won the University of Southampton's Flash Fiction Competition for his story: *Crowman*.

He is also a proud member of the dark fiction writing group: Pen of the Damned.

Literary influences include Friedrich Nietzsche, S. T. Joshi and Russian novelist Andrei Makine.

Dedication

For Christopher Robin, who was so patient,
and provided wine when it was required,
and often when it wasn't.

Acknowledgements

My greatest appreciation to:

Aamer Hussein, Peter Middleton, Alison Fell, Rebecca Smith, Will May, Anna Alessi, Brian and Gillian, for helping me to realise this somewhat strange story.

I must also thank my friends and colleagues at the Coffee Shop, the Hounds of Thirty-One and my fellow Creative Writers in Southampton, for their relentless love and support. My gratitude goes to Philip Hoare, for such encouraging and insightful praise.

And finally to you, the reader, for taking a chance on me and my voice. Without you, the writer is a lonely man or woman. If nothing else, enjoy.

Thomas Brown
June 2013
Oxfordshire

@TJBrown89

'And this also...
has been one of the dark places of the earth.'

Joseph Conrad, *The Heart of Darkness*

CHAPTER ONE

When Freya discovered the pig's remains, on the third of September, they stirred unseemly urges deep inside her. She often circled the village with Eaton, keeping to the surrounding paths, and this day was no different. They passed beneath the alder trees, which grew near Mawley Bog, and around the outskirts of Lynnwood. It was a Sunday, both in name and temperament; an air of sleepiness hung over the village, its inhabitants reluctant to rise, save a nameless few, undaunted by the hour.

As she moved beneath the trees, her thoughts turned to the village's history. There were few in Lynnwood who did not know it well. The village dated back to the fourteenth century when settlers first flocked in real numbers to the Forest, and by all accounts it had changed very little since. Ancient oaks hemmed in the village, and beech and yew and holly. Together they kept the place their own. There was a single bus that went as far as Lymington, which left and returned once each day, and one long, vermicular road. These were the only ways in and out of the village. Many visited the Forest each year, drawn by the herds of wild ponies, the allure of the woodland and its seasonal beauty; the wild gladiolus, found nowhere else in Britain; the carpet of late summer heathers, a sliding scale of purples; even snowdrops, when winter was nigh and the days were at their shortest. It was no wonder that those who ventured into Lynnwood chose to remain. What sane man or woman would want to leave such a place; the sweet, isolating scent of flowering viola, the old Forest paths, the light?

Freya set a brisk pace that morning, her hands buried firmly in her Parka pockets. Tall, dark green wellingtons protected her jeans from the worst of the mud and blonde hair spilled out beneath a faux coonskin cap. It fluttered fiercely in the wind.

The dog, Eaton, caught the scent first and as they broke from the tree line he slipped under the wooden gate, bounding into the adjoining field. At first Freya was unconcerned. Even for a Lurcher, Eaton was a spirited animal. She had bought him for her thirty-fifth birthday, almost eight years ago, and he had been a part of the family ever since. She could only imagine how exciting the world seemed to him and his keen canine senses; the scent of rabbits, of edible things concealed in the grass, even other dogs, a number of which they would usually encounter each morning. Even when she caught an acrid tang on the air, she gave it little thought. McCready must have been burning things. He often ventured into the village, his hands still black, his clothes stinking with smoke.

"What've you found, boy?" she said, smiling into the wind. "Yes, aren't you a clever dog! What's that, then?"

The corpse of the pig stopped her in her tracks. The lingering damp of Mawley Bog was replaced by the smokiness of scorched flesh, which carried on the breeze. Shivering, she brought her hand to her mouth. Fat had bubbled and popped across heat-cracked bone, then cooled in slick, waxy pools between the ribs. Even the surrounding grass was dead; a crisp, ashen elf ring. Flies hovered over the corpse, accountable for the buzzing sound that filled her head as her eyes settled on the skull.

2

It grinned back at her with a sooty, feral smile.

* * *

She left McCready's field quickly, dragging Eaton from the pig by his collar. Arriving home, she first cleaned the dog with a towel. Then she headed upstairs to the bathroom. She wouldn't usually shower after each walk, but that day it felt important. Her skin still shivered, her body unclean, the stink of burned flesh haunting her nostrils.

The blasted pig had deeply unsettled her, but worse were the feelings it had stirred: loathing, fear and the fluttering of hunger. She told herself that she had been mistaken. She had felt a ripple of revulsion, perhaps; the knotting of her stomach at the sight of such a horrid, unexpected thing in the grass, but not hunger! The very thought of bringing her mouth to the charred flesh, of tasting it, cold and crisp on her tongue, was monstrous.

Hot water splashed her skin. For what seemed like the longest time she stood under the spray. Eyes closed, she relished the water as it ran down her body. An antique mirror hung on the opposite wall from the shower, rectangular in shape and framed with golden ornament. Green Men studied her from the frame, their faces wreathed with vines. Her mother had been especially fond of the mirror, and many were the times Freya had stood in the doorway, when just a little girl, watching the older woman as she made herself presentable; hiding the human beneath lipstick and blusher and long, black lashes.

There was no hiding as Freya stepped from the shower, a smudge of exposed pink in the reflection. She glanced at

herself only once, then dressed with her back to the ornament. Birds sang whimsically outside the window while
she clothed herself.

Changed and refreshed – physically, if nothing else –
she returned to the kitchen. She filled the kettle and
prepared a drink, moving stiffly, as though dazed. Eaton
followed her around the room, an auburn shadow at her
feet.

She had not eaten meat since Robert left her. Though
she encouraged her children to eat it, she had not touched
it herself for over ten years. She associated the food with
him and their last meal together, which stuck so vividly in
her mind.

Steam whistled from the kettle's spout like the scream
of burning swine. Moving the kettle from the hob until the
shrill sound trailed off, she poured her tea and drank it.
They said that tea was good for dealing with shock. She
poured another, which she supped more slowly, savouring the sweet warmth that rose from the surface of the
liquid.

* * *

It was a dizzying experience to walk the frosted village in
December. Cobbled pavements were slippery and hard
with ice. The warmth of mulled liquor and brandy burned
throats while the cold weather bit red cheeks. Carollers
moved from cottage to cottage, singing righteous songs in
celebration of the season. Nor were theirs the only voices
to be heard, for the night was Midwinter and on that
night, without fail, the dogs of Lynnwood tossed back
their heads and added their own anxious howls, their

chorus carrying far over the New Forest. The skies were cloudless, the constellation Orion, the Hunter, visible as he chased his quarry through the blackness and the stars.

From the comfort of her front room, Freya watched, as she did every year, a small group of children finish carolling at Granary Cottage across the street. Their failing voices were whisked away by the wind. The ancient hymns made her happy, infusing her with festive spirit. She wasn't a religious woman, like Ms. Andrews of the Vicarage, but it warmed her heart to see the children playing together. They skittered across the icy road, past the parked cars and streetlights to the next cottage, and she turned from the window, the dark silhouette of her reflection doing likewise in the glass.

The house was lively, excitable. An air of anticipation filled the rooms, which she cheerfully attributed to Christmas. Baubles glittered like silvery apples on the potted pine tree in the corner. From the kitchen came the sizzling scent of roast chicken and the crisp, root aroma of potatoes. Her mouth became wet and anxious and she followed the smells and the sounds of cooking to their source.

Where the front room was dim, lit only by lamps and the flickering lights of the tree, the kitchen shone brightly. Exposed oak beams lined the ceiling, an AGA cooker – black from use, even then – dominating the back wall. Robert stood by the dinner table. He stooped to pour two glasses of white, the wine making delicious glugging sounds as it decanted.

"My favourite wine for my favourite woman," he said, turning and pressing a glass carefully into her hand.

"I'm your woman now, am I?"

He grinned, teeth bared in mockery of an ape, and tapped his chest with his fist. "Now and always."

"Misogynist," she said, smiling and sipping from her glass.

"What can I say? I'm an animal."

"You're not the only one." She nibbled his ear as she passed him, her breath sharp and zingy with the white. She tasted it against his lobe and on the air. He shivered bodily between her teeth.

They ate dinner quietly. Even when the dogs began to howl, the peace wasn't ruined. There was something beautiful and primal in the chorus of their cries. She decided then that they should get a dog of their own. He said it was a wonderful idea. Something loyal, to look after their little girl, Lizzie, and recently-born George. Both slept upstairs, lulled by the lingering howls.

It was strange, how well she could recall the details of that meal. Every flavour seemed suffused in her tongue, taste memories; of moist chicken breast, succulent and spiced; of rich gravy, thick and salty; of those hot, slender vegetables, asparagus, still crunchy, and carrots slippery and soft. She ate and drank with abandon, her head thrown back, eyes closed, mouth agape, as if the bestial howls of the dogs erupted from her own throat –

* * *

She didn't see Robert again after that night. Though she could never forgive him for walking out on her, she had loved him once, enough to share a house, a life, to father her children, and the thought of abandoning that drew a roaring panic inside her. Feelings had been unfettered in that field, frightening and seductive, threatening her last memory of her husband with promises of crisp crackling, succulent flesh and dripping grease.

Alone in the kitchen, with only the dog as witness, she stepped slowly towards the black, cast-iron pan, hanging above the hob, and the bottle of cooking oil beside it.

When her children finally dragged themselves downstairs, almost an hour later, they were greeted by the sizzle of hot fat, the splutter of eggs and the rich, salty scent of fried bacon. They smiled sleepily at their mother and seated themselves at the dining table, oblivious to the half-eaten rasher at the bottom of the bin or the guilt behind their mother's eyes.

* * *

Though she did not know it then, Freya was not alone in her private distress. Nor was she the first in Lynnwood to suffer. Ms. Andrews, of the Vicarage, dreamt she saw a woman in the Forest with the face of a fly and great, glassy wings. Mr. Shepherd, at his bench one afternoon, crafted seven intricate brooches, each in the shape of a gaping maw, before he realised what he was doing or how long it had taken him. And McCready was woken one night by screaming. Following the sound to his sties he glimpsed a skeletal figure crouched over the body of one of his pigs. Neck craned to the night sky, it shrieked a ditty from McCready's own childhood:

Scads and 'tates, scads and 'tates.
Scads and 'tates, and conger.
And those who can't eat scads and 'tates,
Oh! they must die of hunger.

These things were not dwelt on. Dreams were disregarded, as dreams so often were, though Ms. Andrews took to wearing her rosary beads beneath the collar of her nightdress while she slept. Mr. Shepherd melted down the ugly, unsettling brooches, except for one, which he secreted into the bottom drawer beside his bed. And once McCready had finished the whisky that he saved for occasions such as this, he dragged the pig's carcass into an empty field, doused it with lighter fluid and burned it. Afterwards, when he woke quite suddenly, sweating and cold in his bed, he couldn't be sure that he had left his pillow at all.

Outside, as a new day broke across the blue autumn sky, the pig's blackened bones cooled in the grass, unobserved by all except one woman and her dog.

CHAPTER TWO

Having felt the playful nip of that hunger, which risked revealing something wild inside her, Freya clung to old habits, finding herself among the village congregation next Sunday. She held no special love for Allerwood Church, but like many of the village's residents she felt a hollowness inside; a quiet corner of her being, forever empty. Some felt this most at night, when their kitchen lights failed them, or when they passed through the Forest in the evening. It was a human thing, she knew, to fear this darkness. Theirs was an epicurean herd, grown fat and contented on life. They had no mind to be stripped of their lives at the trough, by death or any other means.

For others it was dogs that frightened them; the wet stink of their fur, or their animal howls, which carried so easily over Lynnwood. Like the darkness, they reminded of human things; race memories, rank and coppery, best left forgotten. The same swine of society heard the dogs' howls and they buried their faces deeper into their feed, and their lives went on in pleasant Lynnwood.

"The service seems busy this morning," Freya said, when she greeted their vicar, Ms. Andrews, on the church steps that morning.

"Indeed, the promise of winter brings many guilty gluttons to our doorstep." The elderly woman smiled, then winked at Freya's children. "Besides, the more the merrier. We need the bodies."

"I'm sorry?"

"To warm the church, my dear. The building is old as anything in the village. Even filled it doesn't hold heat well."

Darkness held no fear for Freya; she who had been left in the dark already, and there was familiarity in the cries of the dogs that conjured up memories of her last night with Robert, when they had sat at their dining table and eaten to the chorus of howls. Rather, it was the fragility of that memory that kept her awake at night and in a moment of madness, alone in her kitchen, she had threatened that...

She left the old woman to her greetings, leading her children past the alcoves, where there were fewer people to disrupt. They slipped into the third-row pew and waited while the rest of Lynnwood's church-going residents found their seats. The cruciform ground plan was typical of fourteenth-century traditions. Sitting in the third row, she had a clear view of the altar, the high place on which it rested and the transept at the head of the room. There was little of the ornament boasted by grander churches, but theirs was a practical parish. The pews were varnished oak. A table by the entrance held a vase of white-lipped lilies and the collection bowl. White plaster covered the walls and although some stained-glass windows overlooked the nave, these were of a simple design. It was a place of worship and nothing more; a church for a parish which needed spiritual nourishment, when the nights drew in and the dogs began to bay.

Beside her, George fidgeted in his seat. He looked distracted, she thought, as did his sister, their eyes staring but not seeing. She didn't judge them. Church was no place for the wild spirits of children.

"Do I have to come?" Lizzie had said that morning, when Freya stepped into her room and flung open the curtains. The room was dark, stuffy and filled with a menagerie of shapes in the half-light; the products of her daughter's art classes. It smelled of adolescence, and the perfumes used by teenage girls to mask it.

"Yes, darling," she said. "This is family time."

"But it's pointless! You think there's some All-Father sitting up there, nodding when you go to church and frowning when you're bad? You think Dad lived by those beliefs? We're not a parish of medieval sinners. No one believes in God anymore!"

"It doesn't matter what you or anyone else believes," she said, unlocking the window to let some air in. "It's the done thing. The least we can manage is a Sunday, here and there."

"This is stupid," said Lizzie. "Mark Thomas's parents take him to beer festivals, and Rachel's mum cooks her three-course dinners when they need family time. With cheeseboards. And pâté starters."

"You don't like pâté, darling, and neither do I."

"That's not the point," said Lizzie. "You're not listening to me. I'm saying church isn't normal anymore."

"Your skirt's on the bannister," said Freya, unfaltering. "You've got twenty minutes, young lady."

* * *

Freya had heard it said once, when shopping with Robert in Lymington, that the hungry were quick to forget. This was true of the conversation; they were enjoying afternoon tea at a small café and the table beside theirs had entirely forgotten what it was they had ordered. She remembered the café well; the miniature sandwiches filled with wafers of smoked salmon, the lace tablecloths, even the serviettes, printed in patriotic colours and folded carefully for each customer by their place mat. People loved the café, as they loved all places where they could gorge themselves under the pretence of propriety. They were modern predators, snouts speckled not with blood but tea and breadcrumbs.

The saying was also true of Lynnwood, however. Perhaps that was why she had felt such guilt at her appetite, the Sunday she encountered the pig. She could not explain that morning's weakness, which stood against everything she had upheld for over ten years, except that even as she remembered it her mouth began to fill with hot, wet anticipation. For the first time in a decade she had felt temptation, and she had succumbed to it in a moment. They might not be medieval, as her daughter had suggested, but Freya had sinned, and while she continued to sin there was Allerwood Church. The Dark Ages, it seemed, had endured to the twenty-first century, hidden beneath the boughs of the trees and in their hungry hearts.

* * *

The sky was grey and heavy with cloud when they left the service. They took the gravel-stone path through the churchyard and around the back of the church. The little chips made crunching sounds beneath their feet, like hard, dry cereal between her teeth. The three of them moved

12

amid the headstones.

As with most old parishes of its kind, an intimate, if not generous number of graves had sprung up in its grounds over the centuries. The very first graves, the earliest, were those nearest to the church. Some of them were little more than rock piles, their inscriptions long since eroded, or hidden beneath moss. These were the first settlers of Lynnwood, resting beneath its hallowed grounds, from where they might continue to keep a quiet watch over their village. There had been a petition to have the graves restored, she remembered, several years ago. Quite a number of signatures had been gathered from the village's more spiritual residents. They had a more than vested interest in the maintenance of the graves, she supposed, as regular attendees of the church.

Her signature had counted among those collected. She could still recall doe-eyed Ms. Andrews and Sam Clovely from the village council standing on her doorstep that morning; their beatific smiles as they talked to her about heritage, history and remembrance. She had signed, for what it was worth. They weren't bad people and nothing had come of the appeal anyway. Clovely had disappeared one night, halfway through the local campaign, and all the signatures with him. She struggled to remember the details, which were unclear in her mind, but seemed to think they had found a book of his – a journal – in which he had written of noises at his window, late into the night, like the scrabbling of rats or light-fingered children. The general consensus was that he couldn't have been of sound mind, the poor man. The money had gone towards refurbishing the village hall instead, and the leftovers used to fund some cookery classes there. She had attended one with Lizzie, in the spirit of the community. Her daughter seemed to have enjoyed the lesson well enough, though she had found it lacking.

The further they walked from the church, the more recent the graves became. They were still old but their condition gradually improved. They stood higher and straighter in the soil and in many cases the names were still legible where they were engraved into the stone. The most recent dotted the outskirts of the churchyard. The names were still clear, some only a year or two old – if that. They must have been people she knew, to have been buried so recently, and yet she could think of only a handful of people who had passed away in this time. She inspected the family names on the nearest two headstones: Richards and Collins. They meant nothing to her and slipped easily from her mind.

They were almost at the gate when George wandered from the path. She waited while he approached the nearest memorial. For almost a minute he stood in front of the headstone, which was roughly his own height and fashioned after the stony style of its forbears. She couldn't see his face, standing as he was with his back to her, but she watched as he lifted his hand to touch the grey stone. The scene was strangely affecting, stirring something inside of her she couldn't explain. It might have been the sight of one so small, standing alone between the gravestones, or it might have been his fingers on the stone; the living crossing the boundary of the dead. It might have been something obscurer still; her flesh and blood remembering the forgotten. A bouquet of flowers rested at his feet and it brought her some relief to know that someone besides her little boy was caring for the graves. Someone in Lynnwood remembered the buried dead, even if she could not.

CHAPTER THREE

As if that first breakfast had unlocked something inside of Freya, they became a regular habit in the mornings. Any guilt at her activities, the violent shudders of her stomach, faded beneath the sizzling scent of hot fat, the wetness that flooded her mouth and the quick, primitive beating of her heart as she bit into that which was tough and fleshy and once a living, breathing thing. Her lips glistened with grease from swollen sausages and bacon – sometimes rare, other times as crispy and black as that horrid thing melted into McCready's field. The very act of eating became sensual and primal as she remembered that last meal with Robert to be.

Her children remarked on the readiness of cooked breakfasts, and the kitchen stank perpetually of smoke, but beyond that nothing was said. Nothing could be said, for her feasts were private and she always ate alone, before her children woke. The virtue of her vegetarianism was maintained, as was that of her motherhood, and life went on in Lynnwood.

On the thirteenth of September she saw her children, George and Lizzie, return to school. Hollybush Manor was not an outstanding college of learning but it was built, like most of the village's heritage, on old traditions. These aged values gave it strength. It was also blessed with being the only school in Lynnwood. Those children – or indeed their parents – with an appetite for education had nowhere else to turn without driving the distance through the Forest, to Lymington. The school owed much to that hunger.

That morning Freya walked with her children to school. George was more than capable of looking after himself, when left to his own devices, but the other children weren't so accommodating. Only last summer she had been called in for a meeting with his headteacher, Mrs. Morecroft, when it had emerged than Daniel Collins and some of the other boys from George's class were bullying him.

"Good riddance," she said, as they set off from Haven House towards the village green. Nobody had missed the Collins family since they had moved last Christmas. Between their troublesome boy and Mr. Collins's penchant for drink they had made terrible neighbours, undeserving of Lynnwood's good name. She could never remember quite where they had moved to, or the precise date, though truthfully she gave such things little thought.

"I feel sick," muttered George, from where he walked beside her. He refused to hold her hand, no matter where they were, not since his eighth birthday when she had taken him to the park and another boy had laughed at them.

"You feel sick, darling? Where is it, your tummy?"

"Yes, my stomach," he said. "It's cramping."

"Maybe you ate your breakfast too quickly." She paused, crouched to his level and brushed the stray hair from his forehead. "Did you rush your food? You know this happens if you don't chew properly."

From several paces behind them Lizzie snorted. "Maybe you should stop force-feeding us fry-ups every morning."

"Yes," Freya said. "Yes, I... I probably should."

They had stopped on the roadside, by the Old Dairy. The sky stretched pale grey, promising rain. The wind rushed against her face, stinging her cheeks and bringing tears to her eyes. She blinked them dry.

Though the dairy had long since closed down, the field behind it was still used to graze cows. As she watched through the slats in the wooden gate, the nearest lifted its head from the grass and brought its sidelong gaze to bear on her. For several moments she stared at the cow and the cow stared back, its mouth slowly working the cud. And if it seemed as though the cow was chewing something else, something darker, fleshier, as she later thought when she tried to remember what she had seen, she knew that she was mistaken. Cows were herbivores, and largely placid animals at that. They didn't eat meat.

"Hurry up, Mum," said Lizzie, "or we're going to be late. He's not sick, just nervous. I get it all the time when something important's coming up."

"I didn't know that," Freya said.

"Sure you did. That's why I didn't eat before my GCSEs last year, remember?" Shouldering her school bag, her daughter marched ahead.

"Exams or not, you should always eat breakfast, Elizabeth Rankin. It's the most important meal of the day."

"Come on, I think we've all established that much already..."

Presently the grey, moss-flecked brick of the Manor rose into view. Freya knew all about the building, having once helped George with a piece of History homework on the subject. The school was first commissioned in 1698

18

when the wealthy merchant, Peter Young, passed through the village on his way to Lymington. So struck was he by the idyllic air of the village that he committed his thoughts to paper, a modern translation of which could still be read in Southampton's City Library. Freya had found a scan of it on the Internet.

"Knowing the area of the Royal Forest, the New Forest, so well and being so familiar with its surroundings already, which are nothing short of pleasant, I was entirely taken aback by the little village of Lynnwood. I call it a village still, although how it has not yet flourished into something more I cannot fathom. Surely, I challenge anyone who spends more than an evening here, or the day thereafter, to display anything other than reluctance at having to leave this place, or regret at not choosing to stay longer. The soul of this village, its wholesome spirit, is without doubt the public house, The Hollybush. The ale flows freely here, as does the custom, and nary on my travels through the Forest, indeed the county, have I encountered such friendly faces. But there is more to Lynnwood than its tavern. The air tastes clean, unlike that of my London. The cottages are quaint, modest buildings and everywhere I look I find trees, lush and green as any I have ever seen. They must feed well here, and must have done so for many years, to have grown to such heights. Beyond these things, I cannot identify the nature of the village's charm. It is quite plausible this itself is the source of my being contented. An air of underlying pleasantry, which dulls the senses, illuminates everything so softly, and infuses me with a delightful hunger only Lynnwood can appease..."

The children of Lynnwood were at this time educated in the village hall, although poorly and without much in the way of direction. Peter, a firm advocate of the merits of teaching wherever they might be imparted, sought to rectify this and Hollybush Manor was commissioned, named after the pub he had found so charming.

That morning, neither Lizzie nor George was late. She left them to enter the grounds themselves, kissing them both before they went. Then she made the ten-minute walk back to Haven House. She stopped only once, as she passed the field behind the Old Dairy. This time the cows did not stare at her but stood and chewed, as only cows can.

* * *

October became November, the air grew colder, but the Forest still retained the russet glow of autumn. Red leaves clung to the branches, and orange and brown, so that it seemed as though the trees had patchwork quilts draped across the branches. Much of the ground was similarly coloured, where the leaves had started to fall, and the pathways were littered with puddles. These were the best indicators of the subtly changing seasons; even long into the afternoon the puddles retained the icy glaze of morning. Many were cracked, where they had been trodden on, but those that were undisturbed showed no signs of melting. Mawley Bog, when they reached it, was similarly chilled. Sheets of ice spread from the banks across the surface of the water, like hardened wax. Nor was Freya alone in her observations; gone were the swarms of flies, usually seen dancing just above the water level, and the frogs, which seemed to fascinate George so much, were nowhere in sight.

"They're hibernating," he said, when she asked him about their absence. "They crawl into holes beneath the ground and wait out the cold."

She didn't blame the frogs. She had anticipated a mild winter, thrown off, perhaps, by the lingering golden brown of the trees, but walking through the Forest she knew she had been mistaken. There was nothing mild about the air. Her faux coonskin cap protected her ears, and she had even seen need for a scarf.

They took the long route around the water. Of the two ways around Mawley Bog, this was the path her parents had always preferred. Often her father would take her for walks but sometimes her mother, Harriet, accompanied them.

* * *

Freya chased the dogs beneath the trees. The year was '76 and she was nine years old. Though her chest heaved and her feet flew, her legs were only little. The dogs barked playfully as they dashed ahead, noses close to the ground. The earth was a spill of shadows and soil.

"Careful, Freya, darling, don't run too far!"

She didn't heed her mother's advice. It was a wonder she heard it at all. The Forest was not Haven House. Propriety held no sway here, only sharp branches and soft leaves and the damp Forest mulch beneath her shoes. Here she could run as fast as she wanted, as far as she wanted, with her faithful hounds by her side.

"David, she's going to hurt herself."

"Let her run," he said. His voice seemed to carry through the trees. "She knows to keep to the paths. And look at her, look at that smile. Have you ever seen her so happy?"

"She's easily pleased. Unlike her mother."

David's voice thawed into laughter. "You're telling me."

"You'd hardly think we were related, looking at her now. A wild child of the Forest."

"Oh, I don't know about that. Look at how her hair streams behind her. And her cheeks, when she turns around. Tell me you don't recognize those cheeks..."

Freya's parents continued talking until they faded out of earshot. Still she ran after the dogs. Exhilaration burned her chest as Ralph and Jack led her deeper into the trees. They came upon the hollow of an oak, where leaves had fallen, or been blown into a pile. She slipped between the dogs, kneeling before the hollow. It felt colder here, though not unpleasant. The air smelled ripe. Poking through the leaf-layer, like a child's emerging tooth, was a small bone. She touched it tentatively at first, feeling the smoothness of the creamy surface, dry and light. Then she grasped it firmly and pulled it from its bed of leaves; a tool with which to repulse her mother and impress her father. How proud he would be of his brave little girl! How her mother would shriek!

* * *

Harriet had been a vain woman, the product of modernity, but even she hadn't been able to ignore the allure of the Forest, as though some part of her under that

22

false face longed to be beneath the trees. It was a longing that had kept her from the Forest, in the same way that the hungry sometimes deny themselves food, for fear of overindulgence. Freya knew that now, although such a thing would never have occurred to her younger self, who only delighted that both her parents were walking with her. She drew comfort from that delight, from the old paths, the memories of simpler times.

She wrapped that comfort round her like a blanket. More than the cold or the arrival of winter she detected something else in the Forest; a gnawing uneasiness at the back of her mind. She didn't see or hear anything untoward, but she couldn't deny the weight she felt, pressing in from all around.

"What's that?" George said suddenly. Lost in her thoughts, she had almost walked into him. He was standing in the middle of the path. She followed where he was pointing to a bird, a solitary magpie, perched on a sign.

"That's a magpie, George."

"No, not the magpie. I know what those are," he said. "I meant the other thing."

"What other thing?" She studied the Forest.

"There was a figure, by the trees. A person, I think, except it was hard to see properly because of the shade."

"It was probably another person then," she said. "You know, plenty of people from the village walk their dogs around here, like we do."

"It reminded me of someone. My friend from the train tracks."

"Your friend?"

23

He looked up at her with wide, impressionable eyes, the darkness of the Forest reflected in his pale face. "My friend. The man who lives in the tunnel."

* * *

The memories are so clear now. She can hardly think, hardly breathe, for their clarity, after so long in the dark. That which was once clouded has run clear until she can think of nothing else. They sluice like the brook through her mind, its waters swollen with spring.

She pauses, pen in hand, and turns to the AGA cooker. The ache inside her redoubles, crippling in its intensity until she cannot move except to clutch her arms around her stomach. But these are not hunger pangs; they are aches of a different kind. It is not her stomach wrapped in her arms but her abdomen and the womb beneath, where her little ones first came into being, where they grew and from where they were born into this wilderness world. They are children of Lynnwood and now Lynnwood has them again. She feels hollow. Light-headed at the thought of what they have become. They are lost to her, devoured by the same hunger that threatens to consume their mother.

She moans helplessly, a low, bovine sound, before dropping her pen and clasping a hand to her mouth. Her eyes flicker to the window. Evening is fast fading. Shadows lengthen, spilling from the empty windows of Granary Cottage opposite, moving where all else is still. The building is tinged with the lingering pink of dusk. Soon there will be shadows of other things too; bony silhouettes peering into her house, crawling through the streets, slender arms reaching for her door. And she will answer them. She will open her house to Midwinter because there is no fighting it anymore...

There is not long left but there is still time, if she writes quickly. She retrieves the pen from the tabletop and places the nib to paper. With the smells of the Forest filling her nostrils and the haunting laughter of her children in her ears, she writes.

CHAPTER FOUR

The more that she ate, the more she surrendered to those instincts she had for so long been conditioned against, and the more she began to remember. It was a therapy of food; slim rashers of crisp pig, bursting sausages, eggs beaten to within an inch of their lives by her practised hands, as though not eggs but something else, transformed into dripping omelettes. It was only natural, she supposed, that these memories manifested in her dreams at first. What else are dreams, but memories of the past, the future; of what could have been, or might yet be?

* * *

She dreamt first of the Forest. She couldn't see the brook from where she walked but she could hear it; a lively rushing of water through the trees. It was dark here, but not oppressively so; light broke through the dense canopy in wide pools, which scattered the shadows of the forest floor. Occasionally the path would take her through a glade or clearing, where more light reached, uninterrupted by leaves or branches. It must have been summer; delicate elf rings dotted the grass, inviting her to run through them, to jump from circle to circle, and dandelion seeds drifted languidly on the air.

Another figure moved behind her in the Forest. She could feel his presence; the press of his footfalls on the ground. She knew without looking that it was her father and that she was a little girl. The trees were taller, so much taller than she remembered them being, the grass much closer to her face. Wood pigeons warbled softly in the trees, as did a number of birds she couldn't identify. She didn't suppose it mattered; the birds sang and the forest air was pleasant. These were the important things. This, surely, was why the memory had endured, hidden for so many years. She felt dizzy with nostalgia.

Father and daughter moved deeper into the Forest. She saw other shapes now, twin shadows in the undergrowth: their two Cocker Spaniels, Ralph and Jack. The dogs moved through the shrubs without stopping, their noses never far from the ground. Occasionally they would collide, as the same scent brought them together. Playful yelps ensued, scattering through the trees, followed by laughter. She realised it was her own, and that she was smiling.

The brook drew closer. She could see the gap ahead, where the trees grew slightly apart, and she hurried towards it. She moved faster now. She seemed to be skipping.

Bauchan Brook, named after a local legend of Lynnwood, said that visitors to the water were watched by someone or something between the trees; a spirit of the wilds or perhaps the trees themselves, standing guard over the clear waters from which they drank. She had no such memories, no encounters that she could recall, but she couldn't deny the presence that hovered over the place; a quiet watchfulness, seeming both young and old.

Except, this time when she stepped from the tree line, as she knelt to dip her hands into the water, she thought she did see something. A silhouette, crouched across the brook. She saw only its reflection first, broken and pale in the shining waters. Filled with curiosity she looked up, the figure across the brook doing likewise. Their eyes met and she felt a deep, irrepressible urge inside of herself, the likes of which she had never felt before. Then the brook seemed to expand, breaking its banks as the light washed down through the trees, and the trees themselves rose taller and thinner until there was nothing but that shining, liquid light and she woke, wet and hot, in bed.

* * *

Though Freya never actually saw her father in these dreams, he wasn't far from her thoughts. David Heart was as shrewd a businessman as he was a devoted father, and he had always been there for his daughter.

"He was tall. And broad. I remember him being broad," said Catherine, her eyes sparkling devilishly over a glass of white one afternoon. "Big, strong arms."

"Catherine Lacey. You're awful, do you know that?"

"Would you have me any other way?"

Despite growing up in the same school year as Freya, Catherine still seemed the more youthful of the pair. Her rotund face concealed age, and her portly figure, with her thick neck and generous arms, suggested a volup-tuousness Freya's slender shape lacked. Even so, the two remained as close friends as they had ever been. Where they had run through the heathland as little girls, now Freya's dog gambolled over the grass. The poetry they had read at school filled Catherine's bookcases. One collection comprised of Catherine's own verse, though Freya had been forbidden from ever reading it. And the squash that they used to drink had become darker, stronger and much more alcoholic in nature, though they drank it with no less relish. Catherine had always possessed something of a nose for "the good stuff", ever since they first started sneaking bottles from her parents' wine cellar after school. Raised on these fumes, it was only natural that the woman had grown up with a taste for them.

"I've been thinking a lot about him lately," said Freya, staring over her glass into the garden. "About what happened to him, the unfairness of it. The disease took everything from him. That business was his life."

"Everything! Remind me, did the business fail?"

"Well, no," said Freya. "He sold his shares long before the end. There was no other way. He couldn't run a company with dementia."

"There we go," said Catherine. "The wheels of industry kept turning. Some poor soul will have risen to replace him and that was the end of it, as far as they were concerned."

"You're saying his business lived on without him. Is this supposed to be comforting?"

"Yes! Consider that Sam Clovely. He took his seat on the village council so seriously, but what good did it actually do him?"

"He was mad, Catherine..."

"No, he went mad." She rolled her eyes. "When you get down to it, it's not work that matters, it's not job titles or a place at the head of the business table. These things go on regardless. It's Haven House. It's your memories. It's you."

"Me?"

"You, your father's seed, his flesh and blood –"

"You're growing vulgar again," said Freya, winking. "It's too early in the evening for that yet."

"Dress it up however you like." Catherine took a large mouthful of her wine. "You know what I mean. There's working and there's living."

Birdsong sounded from the garden. It was light, without worry. Freya watched as one of Catherine's cats stalked a sparrow through the undergrowth. "I've been dreaming about him again," she said.

"Your father?"

She nodded and Catherine smiled wickedly.

"I've been dreaming about him too. What would your mother have said?"

The cat sprang, the sparrow vanishing beneath its claws.

* * *

When not in Catherine's company, Freya found herself increasingly drawn to Allerwood Church. She had lived a privileged life, all things considered. Her father worked hard to provide for his family and she had inherited generously on her parents' passing. She visited the churchyard in the afternoons, once Eaton had been walked and the children were at school. The dreams gnawed at her resolve, their little teeth nipping at wounds long since healed until they were red and raw.

"It is clear you have something on your mind, my dear," said Ms. Andrews, after they had exchanged pleasantries one afternoon. The vicar made her way through the graves, to stand by Freya's side.

"Is it so obvious?"

"Indeed," said Ms. Andrews. "I have a view of the church grounds from my windows. It's really quite beautiful, in the summer. Pardon my saying, but you're spending near as much time here as the dead. Is there anything I can help you with?"

"I don't think so. Thank you, though."

"You are sure, Freya? God is healing, you know, and failing that I have an excellent brandy in need of drinking."

"I feel... I'm remembering things, that's all."

A curious look passed over Ms. Andrews's face at these words. The woman seemed suddenly older and younger, almost childlike in her expression. She toyed with her hands behind her back.

"We're all remembering things. Winter, it seems, has brought a host of memories this year." She stared into middle-space for a moment, her wet eyes glistening. Then she smiled. "Come inside, let us talk and eat."

CHAPTER FIVE

Shadows and a vacuous quiet filled the Vicarage with a rigid presence that seemed, momentarily, to still the waking hunger inside Freya.

With shaking hands, Ms. Andrews unscrewed a dusty bottle and poured two splashes of amber coloured liquid into glasses. The old woman sat across from her in the drawing room, which had the same stale air, Freya thought, as Allerwood Church. An effort had been made to soften the room and make it more hospitable, but not a great one. Varnished elm bookcases lined the walls, filled with volumes of texts, and a vase of lilies wilted on the windowsill. A plate of scones filled the table between the two women, small pots of jam and cream beside it. The smell of brandy blossomed in the room.

"Lynnwood is an old village," said Ms. Andrews, sipping slowly from her glass. "The old ways still hold sway here, though there are few who see it."

"Yes, we have a longstanding heritage here –"

"I see it, though," she went on. "I notice these things. I know what to look for, especially of late. So I realise the importance of our church here in Lynnwood."

"What do you mean?"

She indicated wildly to the bookcases, a drop of liquor spilling from her glass. Again, she did not seem to notice. "There are books, parchments and diaries here, which date back to the earliest days of the village. There are still more in the study. I have read many, although it would take another lifetime to read them all. These matters interest me."

They sat in silence for some minutes. Freya expected Ms. Andrews to continue, to expand on her observations, but she seemed distracted, her eyes fixed over her drink. Freya had a short sip of her own brandy, which tasted as it had smelled, then prepared her scone out of politeness. They were freshly baked, she noted, probably bought at market that morning.

She was spreading jam when Ms. Andrews chose to speak again.

"We didn't always have such comforts. Those early days were dark ones. I was unsurprised when I learned our church was among the first of the buildings to be fashioned here."

"I had read similarly –"

"People always turned to God in those times. He was a means of coping, a source of spiritual strength, a means, they thought, of elevation from the beasts of the earth."

Freya was surprised at the note of disdain in the vicar's voice. "You think this has changed?"

"Of course it has, Freya. People don't come to church anymore, not for God anyhow. I'm not sure if they ever really did come for Him. People's reasons are generally their own."

Freya felt herself blushing, but nodded and took another hurried sip of alcohol. It stung her tongue and cheeks.

"But enough of that," said Ms. Andrews. "Tell me, what is it you remember?"

Warm and liberated by brandy and the frankness of her host, she recounted to Ms. Andrews honestly the dream that had filled her sleeping thoughts for over a week now.

All the time that she spoke, the old woman watched her, nodding occasionally. Otherwise she was silent. Those loose, watery eyes stared right into her own, unafraid; an adult, listening to the anxieties of a child. Encouraged, Freya then spoke of her uneasiness, of the unrest she sensed in Lynnwood.

"It is strange that you dream of the Forest," Ms. Andrews said finally, when she had heard everything.

"Is it?"

"Yes, you see, I too have been dreaming of it. Not memories, or pleasant, energetic dreams, as yours sound, but dreams all the same."

The words that spilled from Ms. Andrews's mouth that afternoon took firm, wild root in Freya's head. She talked of horrible things, made all the more so for the righteous voice that spoke them. Freya couldn't help but worry for the troubled mind that formed such fantasies, or worse, endured them, night on night.

* * *

Ms. Andrews's dream was always the same; a woman with a housefly face and wings like stained church glass. Only each time she dreamt it was longer and longer before she woke from them. No matter how much she prayed when she rose each morning, or how softly she appeared to sleep, it was the same. And as her dreams deepened, playing out longer in her mind, she found herself approaching this figure in the Forest. She was helpless to move otherwise, no matter how much she struggled to turn, to run back through the trees, to the Vicarage and home.

The figure under the trees was a horrible sight to behold. Ms. Andrews had thought she had seen her fair share of suffering in her life-time; her sermons preached often of lepers and she had worked with other, more unfortunate souls during the years of her service. But this woman, if she could even be called such, was by far the most abhorrent. Each night that Ms. Andrews dreamt, the figure took a step closer, and each night a little more of her became visible under the fading light.

Smooth, supple curves made up her human parts; pale, Elizabethan skin, soft and naked. Her legs were long but well-proportioned, her hips broad, as Sarah's, blessed mother of Isaac. Then she saw the face of the woman, her large head that of a housefly, like the ones that crawled behind the curtains in the drawing room to die. Its flesh was mottled and leathery and its eyes were like fractured glass, or, she thought, morality, from the way that it looked at her; a thousand glittering facets, strangely human, staring from across the clearing.

And most unsettling to Ms. Andrews was that each step across the forest floor brought the uneasy apparition itself closer. Every step that she took was mirrored by the horrid, fly-shaped figure opposite; until she knew one evening they would meet.

It was always with this realisation, she said, that she woke, sweating, damp and with a thirst only alcohol would slake.

* * *

Every resident of Lynnwood knew its vicar, though few found need to call Joan Andrews by her first name. A polite, private woman to meet, this changed when she preached, as if in doing so she was forced to expend herself, to draw deep from within. The lessons of her life became the subject of her sermons. And they were righteous speeches. Her voice, deceptively strong for one so physically frail, carried far over the pews.

Freya had sat through more than enough of these sermons to piece together the old woman's past, without their own private conversations taken into consideration. The rarer details of her history were imparted over cream tea and drink, such as they had taken the afternoon they discussed their dreams, and if she was an outspoken woman with a long life story to share, brandy only served to loosen her tongue.

Ms. Andrews was born and bred of the village. Christ was in her blood, she said; passed down from her father, and his father before him. She was the first and last woman in her lineage to take the title as vicar of Lynnwood. She had never seen fit to marry and, at seventy one, was childless.

There had been one man in her life, beside the Lord himself; a Frederick Mangel, travelling from Brittany the summer of '63. Already in Normandy visiting family, it had been the small matter of a ferry across the waters and he was among the Forest. He had remained in Lymington for three days before venturing deeper into the trees. It was his purpose to see as much of the place as he could; he had desired to visit for many years and, with business growing – he ran a small recruitment agency – he doubted he would have the time again for months to come.

On the fourth day he discovered Lynnwood and that, as

Ms. Andrews put it, was that. A Romanticist at heart, he found an intense, spiritual satisfaction in the dappled light of the trees, the intoxicating freshness of the air, the carefree birdsong in the branches.

Ms. Andrews first met him in the churchyard while laying flowers by the headstones. He asked her to dinner. She accepted and they ate matelote, which he cooked himself using fish from Bauchan Brook. She could not remember ever having eaten such delicious food and it was true to say she melted somewhat under the warmth of that sharp cider stew.

It wasn't meant to last, however. That very Christmas – on the twenty-first, to be exact – he excused himself politely from dinner, citing reasons she couldn't since recall. She couldn't remember seeing him leave the Vicarage, or whether he had packed any clothes. All she did know was that she never saw him again. He flashed behind her eyes sometimes, when the dogs howled or the winter air rattled at the windows. All other times he was a shadow. A ghost of her past. He had proposed only three days prior to his leaving and, against every doubt, every pang of uncertainty, she had said yes.

That, she confessed over a glass or three of mulled wine two winters ago, was her one regret. She had been quite tipsy at the time and the confession had brought tears to both of their eyes, for Ms. Andrews deserved better. She was mild-mannered but stern, loving but fair, and charitable. When she encountered those people down on their luck, drinkers and the homeless, she would often sit and talk with them. Sometimes she gave them her blessings and when she prayed they were never far from her thoughts. Such charity, she said, cost nothing.

It was this grounded sensibility, this honesty and good nature, that endeared her to Freya and ensured that, when she voiced her unsettling dream, Freya listened. These were not the ravings of a mad old woman. Ms. Andrews was no Dickensian spinster, no matter her circumstances. And had they been ravings, she would have humoured them with her time anyway. Joan Andrews deserved that much.

CHAPTER SIX

One week to the day since her conversation with Ms. Andrews, Freya found herself on the banks of Bauchan Brook. She stared out over the brook for several minutes, watching the rushing waters run their course. They leapt and fell in smooth, undulating motions, curving around pebbles, sparkling in the afternoon light. Though bright, the air was still very cold, her gloved hands finding homes in her pockets. The sound of running water filled her ears. More than once, she thought she heard voices on the wind, of far-off people talking between the trees.

She had continued to gorge herself each morning. These feasts were without conscience; she ate until her jaw ached, her stomach turned and her hands were slick with grease. It was the grease that she craved so much. Even after finishing, if it could ever be called such when she was always left so dissatisfied, she would lick her fingers clean, sucking the fleshy flavours from them until there was nothing left to taste.

At first she would cook the food. Such civilised habits were hard to break, even in the throes of abandon. But as days became weeks and her appetite grew, so her impatience grew with it. There was no tolerance in gluttony, after all; no lenience, no admirable qualities of any kind. It was a dark pit of self-gratification, from which the hungriest figures clambered forth with ravenous intent. In her impatience she forwent the act of cooking. The kitchen became a different place then; filled with the wet, bestial sound of chewing as Freya tore into raw meat and other such foods however she could find them. It was into this kitchen that George tumbled, the morning he almost caught her.

* * *

Neck-deep in the refrigerator, only half-aware of her son's sudden presence in the doorway, Freya froze. She spoke to him without turning, raw egg spilling from her lips.

"You're up early today and on a Sunday, too."

"Couldn't sleep," he said, moving to stand behind her. She felt his hand as he tugged at her dressing gown. "What's for breakfast?"

"You couldn't sleep?" She swallowed down the gelatinous albumen, before too much of it escaped her mouth. The rest she wiped on the back of her sleeve. "Why couldn't you sleep, huh?"

"The man from the tunnel keeps coming to my room."

She struggled to remember, to place his words. They came to her slowly, as if through a dream, a parting veil. "Your friend?"

"He's not my friend anymore."

"Don't worry, darling," she said, turning and hugging him tightly. He stood quite rigid while she embraced him. "Nightmares aren't real. They can't hurt you."

"I know. What's for breakfast?"

"What would you like for breakfast?" she said.

He seemed to think about this. "Eggs?"

"We're fresh out," she said, standing and swallowing. "How about some cereal, does that sound good?"

He shrugged and seated himself at the table.

It was a bright November morning, most of the clouds having rained themselves out the night before. Sunlight streamed in through the kitchen window, cold but pleasant, catching the raindrops that lingered on the glass. It promised to be a lovely day. The perfect weather for a walk through the Forest.

"What were you doing?" George said, watching her from the table.

"When?"

"Just now, when I walked in."

She frowned, opened her mouth to speak, then thought the better of it. "Waking up," she said, smiling. "Just waking up."

"You were eating raw eggs," he said.

"Don't be silly, darling. People don't eat raw eggs."

"It's all down your sleeve and at the end of your chin."

She moved into the hallway and examined her face in the mirror there. A string of cloudy egg white hung from her chin, like saliva from a dog's mouth.

"I don't know..." she started hesitantly. Wiping her face clean, she returned to the kitchen. "I can't remember." Then, more certainly: "You shouldn't eat raw eggs, George. Some of them contain salmonella. That's a disease that you can catch from certain foods, if they're not cooked properly."

"I know I shouldn't. And I know what salmonella is, I read about it in a book. And you were eating raw eggs. There's evidence."

She heard Lizzie on the stairs; the last three always creaked, then her daughter was standing in the doorway.

"Morning, Mum..."

"Morning, darling."

"What's for breakfast?"

"Not eggs," said George. "Mum's eaten them all."

"I haven't eaten any eggs, George!"

"I don't mind, except that you have and it's not very safe."

Lizzie crossed the kitchen, also in her dressing gown, and seated herself opposite her brother. "Eggs aren't unsafe. They're really good for you."

"Not when they're eaten raw, as Mum likes them."

"George, enough!" snapped Freya.

"Mum!" said Lizzie, "what the hell?"

Slamming the refrigerator door shut, Freya rounded on the dining table. "I haven't been eating raw eggs. The consumption of raw eggs isn't advisable and I never want to see either of you risking your health that way. Understood?"

Silence settled over the kitchen. She stared at her children and they stared back. Outside, from the back garden, two blackbirds took up song, broken only by a single, delicate crack, as an egg rolled from the work surface to the floor.

"I'm going back to bed," said Lizzie.

"You haven't eaten anything," said Freya.

"Not hungry." Lizzie rose and left the kitchen.

George began swinging his legs, in time to the blackbirds' chirps. "What cereal have we got?"

* * *

It had been a long time since she had born witness to the brook in the flesh. She had stopped coming here after her father had died. It hadn't felt right, walking the paths they had walked together without him. She could still remember the tales he used to tell, which had so frightened and fascinated her as a child...

The wind whispered louder in her ears and she fancied it was the Forest's voice telling her those stories again; of the Bauchan, who haunted the hungry waters, luring careless young girls to their wild, watery deaths in the brook of its namesake, and how it would claim her, too; if she strayed too far from the paths.

Such tales were nonsense, of course; stories concocted to keep children safe, if not obedient. She had lived long enough to know the power of fear. Their society was built on it and the order it maintained. She thought this was what Ms. Andrews had meant, when they had spoken in her drawing room. The church upheld peace. It promised life everlasting to the good, the docile. And those who strayed from the path... She had only to open the pages of a Bible to read these things; the eternal damnation that awaits the immoral, the armies of Sin that plagued the land and other Christian legends. There still existed statues of those same Sins in the churchyard; fickle creatures, so much like men and women but twisted and monstrous as the vices they personified.

Fear fulfilled its purpose. Her father had told her these things not to scare her but to keep her safe. In Southampton and London, children were taught the dangers of traffic, of unsafe streets and knife-crime. Their urban Bauchan went by other names; Rawhead and Bloody Bones, Jack the Ripper, the Bunny Man. Even now, younger, no-less horrible apparitions existed, the urban legends of today. Fear was nurtured, fed like an appetite, until it had grown into something bloated and undying.

Reaching for a stone, she tossed it underarm into the brook. It vanished instantly beneath the rushing waters, but she continued to stare after it, deep in thought. Lynnwood's dangers were different, of course, but no less cautionary. They warned of older things, more insidious than traffic or knife-crime; those of the wild woods, of becoming lost, of drowning beneath the trees.

Instead of visiting the brook alone, she had played behind the Old Barn with the other children. She had gone to church, walked the safe places and lived a good life. Without fear and the order it maintained they were little better than the beasts of the Forest.

* * *

As the afternoon wore on she wandered even further down the brook. She wasn't sure what she had expected, as she followed the delicate music of the water downstream. A torrent of memories, a welling of emotion, the Bauchan, thin and hungry, standing opposite her on the bank...

She smiled to herself as she wandered by the shallows. Her father would have encouraged her to return here. It wasn't a place to fear anymore but somewhere pleasant, somewhere genuine and beautiful. She vowed to come again soon, with the children. Lizzie would love the visual spectacle of the brook; the sheets of broken ice that covered the banks, the sluice of the currents, the dead leaves, which were swept helplessly away. And as she walked with George she would speak to him in hushed tones of the Bauchan, and the legend of this particular forest spirit would live on through the telling, as it had done for so long already.

It occurred to her, as she shouted for Eaton through the trees, that this might have been the reason for her dreams. They were calling her, as readily as she summoned the dog, back to the wild waters and the place of her memories. Dreams were one thing, but even their lucidity could not match the brush of the breeze against her face, the glittering brook in the afternoon light, the roughness of the bark when she dragged her fingers over the trees.

Eaton broke from the undergrowth and pottered into the shallows. His fur was matted with burrs and sticks but it was the bird in his mouth that drew her eyes and held them; a magpie, chewed almost beyond recognition, iridescence flashing from its tail-feathers.

Wincing at the sight, she bent to retrieve the poor bird, only half aware that, distorted by the currents, her reflection might have been grinning as it stooped to snatch the dog's prey from his mouth.

* * *

That evening, at dinner, George wept over the fate of the magpie. There was no escaping the influence of the Forest; the rank, metallic breath of mortality. They were all mercy to the wild whims of the trees, which could one moment bear them to peaceful epiphany, even as they cast their chill shade over Lynnwood.

George disclosed to her that evening that he had only two friends in Lynnwood, the first of whom was a magpie, which had that very afternoon failed to show at its perch for the first time in nearly a year. And what horror – his face pale, small lips quivering, mouth agape with something else than hunger. More familiar than most his age with the harsh brevity of life – the insects he admired lived brittle, brutal existences – the death of this bird represented something entirely different. His grief was a testament to the loneliness she had always worried he felt, but had never before admitted to herself.

George often wandered down by the old train tracks, tracing the line through the Forest. All manner of insects made the tarnished metal sleepers their home and he went there to hunt for them beneath the rotted wood beams and cold, dew-slicked sleepers. This, he said, was where the magpie lived, where they met each afternoon at around three o'clock, when he finished school for the day.

The line had been important once, linking Lynnwood to Brockenhurst and, from there, the rest of the county. Built in the 1890s, it had meant a great deal to Lynnwood, which had until then been isolated by the very Forest that sustained it. The line had brought the first meaningful waves of visitors to the village, opening it up to Hampshire. For all its benefits it had not lasted. Lynnwood seemed incapable of supporting the industrial intrusion; the Forest unwilling to tolerate such a hungry competitor. The Old Places were so often indifferent to change, Freya knew. The Oldest seemed almost opposed to it.

The bird would always greet George from where it perched, on the rotten remains of its tree. He said its tree, not because it nested there or ever had done, to his knowledge, but because that was where it waited. Indeed, it never seemed to move from the spot, except to cross the clearing, or settle nearer to him as he moved down the track. Occasionally it would emit a gleeful croak; a raucous sound, like the rattling wings of a giant cicada. He hadn't named the bird. What difference did a name make except to belittle something, to make it less than it actually was? Its scientific title was *Pica pica*, he knew, not entirely dissimilar from the sound it made, and that was enough for him.

A keening sadness sprang inside of Freya as her son recounted these things, but he seemed genuinely happy in his own company. Nor did he know any better. Perhaps that was his saving grace; a wild streak, that of the lone hunter, sparing him the heartache of solitude. Even as she thought this, she knew it wasn't true; why else would he be brought so low by the death of the bird, unless it had meant something to him? Through these sobering realisations she began to perceive the nature of her son more clearly.

They were eating roast chicken at the dinner table when he learned the horrid news. The cooked bird was golden and large, served with all the trimmings. This in itself had caused a quiet stir between her children; Freya hadn't sat down to a roast with them in living memory.

"You're not eating very much," she said to Lizzie between forkfuls.

"And you're eating chicken," replied Lizzie.

"I'm making an effort," she said, feeling herself redden before her children. Steam pressed heavily against the inside of the windows in dripping, opaque smears. She thought quickly, then realised she needn't lie. "I haven't been feeling myself recently."

"Me neither," replied her daughter. "Too many fry-ups.

They're making me sick."

The kitchen fell silent, disturbed only by the slow scrape of cutlery on plates. She tried to concentrate, to counter her daughter, but found her thoughts numbed by the rich aromas of the food. Instinct swelled under those scents, pressing against her chest, filling her mouth with juices. Inside, she screamed to throw herself across the table, to take up great handfuls of food, to tear the legs from the chicken and force them into her open mouth, so hungry, so desperate to be filled –

Somehow, she held herself in check. Instead she sat quite still, contenting herself with one forkful at a time.

Almost automatically, to fill the silence as much as reclaim some sense of self, of civility, she recounted the events of her day, and it was then, as she mentioned Eaton and the magpie, that her son's face fell and the truth of his circumstances came tumbling out. With them came his tears, uncharacteristic as her appetite for meat.

* * *

The nib of her pen buries into the page. Her hand is shaking, her fingers white as the sheets of paper beneath. Words seem to have momentarily lost meaning and there is nothing but the memory of her son's face; tear-stained at the upheaval of death, of the wild spirit leaving that magpie's body, its cold, decaying remains, left to be devoured by the dogs and the beetles.

His face shines before her eyes, so pale, so vulnerable, and her chest heaves; a generous, violent movement. Then she swallows, as if consuming the memories might make them leave, as it has made everything else disappear. It is not what has become of her son that upsets her; she knows he is in a better place. She sees that now. He is wild, free as the magpie to which he was so endeared; to move between the trees, the light, the dark, to relish in unbridled freedom beneath the vast sky, to run and hunt and eat as appetite desires...

But she misses him. The emotion endures because, like the hunger, it is instinct. She realises that now. Her son as she knew him is gone. She is nothing to him, or he to her, except memories, and soon even they will be devoured.

Except for the ones recorded by the fading light, in dark blue ink across the half-filled pages beneath her.

CHAPTER SEVEN

The morning Freya accompanied Ms. Andrews to the Forest was the last time she, or anyone else in Lynnwood, ever saw the old woman.

Ms. Andrews's dreams had been growing worse, she confessed after service the following Sunday. There was no escaping the fly-faced woman or the nightly visitations that brought her closer. She felt constantly drained and had taken to drinking herself into a stupor each evening. This, she discovered, was the only way to ensure a restful night, if alcohol-induced sleep could ever be called such. True to her words, the woman's breath burned with brandy. Her eyes were shallow pits in her face and her frame had shrunk, so that she resembled a wrinkly child or the husk of one of George's insects, left too long in the damp. The woman seemed to have aged years in a matter of weeks.

The sky was bleak; a vast expanse of distance, grey and empty except for the thin wind, which howled through the church corridors. They were standing just outside the entrance, on crumbling stone steps, and could hear the wind clearly as it sang through the building.

"Another insightful service," Freya said, "thank you again, Joan. What would we be without you?"

"You mean where, surely?" said the vicar, laughing.

"Yes, of course! Still, thank you."

"You're welcome. It's always a pleasure to see familiar faces gathered in one place. How are you keeping?"

"I visited the brook," said Freya, "after we last spoke."

"That's good, my dear. How do you feel?"

"I didn't mean to walk by that way. I just sort of ended up there. Looking back, my father wouldn't have wanted me to avoid it for so long. It really is beautiful this time of the year."

"I'm pleased to hear you're feeling better," said Ms. Andrews.

"It'll be the same for you, with the clearing in the Forest. Think of it as therapy."

As Ms. Andrews heard this, a curious expression swept her face. She gasped silently, like a fish left to die on the banks of the brook. She recovered quickly. "I'm not so sure I should follow in your footsteps. My dreams are not of your pleasant sort."

"Then, if anything, a visit to the trees will remind you."

"Remind me?"

"Well, that the Forest is not as you dream it." Freya smiled encouragingly as the two moved away through the graveyard. "We'll go together. Tomorrow, once the children have left for school. Eaton will need walking anyway."

After a moment of hesitation, Ms. Andrews returned a thin smile. "Yes, of course. Who am I, refusing the prospect of company on a Monday morning? I have a number of errands to run anyway. It will be good to catch up properly, and see that beautiful dog of yours."

"He's a wild spirit," she said, her laughter carrying over the graves.

"Aren't we all?" said Ms. Andrews. "Aren't we all?"

* * *

They met earlier than planned that Monday morning,

Freya having also found errands to run. These were not dissimilar to Ms. Andrews's own and, after browsing the high street for almost an hour, they headed to McCready's farmhouse. The morning was misty with frost, the village cobbles treacherous. Cold light filtered through the clouds, which rolled like crashing waves through the sky. The air stung her cheeks and numbed her nose; winter, teasing her flesh with its teeth.

They made polite conversation as they moved towards the Old Barn. Freya spoke much of Lizzie and George; their art projects and school progress respectively. A great deal of fuss was made over Eaton, who was more than happy to oblige their attentive hands by presenting his belly and the backs of his ears. Ms. Andrews seemed well enough, although she still looked disturbed at the prospect of entering the Forest. Freya understood, given the lucidity of her own dreams. If Ms. Andrews's horrible visitations were anything similar, her apprehension was not unfounded.

Freya thought only of the healing to be found there, or if not healing then a freedom from the pressures of the village, of life, a primitive release. The delicate sound of the water as it ran its course, the rich aroma of bark, the feel of the Forest as it snapped beneath her wellies; Ms. Andrews would experience these things for herself, she would unbridle whatever beasts strained within and, relieved of these burdens, sleep would once again become restful.

The wind picked up as they approached McCready's farmhouse. Although she could see no smoke behind the barn or in the fields, she fancied she could smell the charred pig again, or the ghost of that smell, clinging stubbornly to her nostrils and the wet slip of her tongue; a smoky-lipped lover, pressing the taste into her mouth...

Moving past the barn, which seethed with the clamour of livestock; the metal sounds of riled fencing, bestial snorts and the clatter of unsettled trotters, they reached the farmhouse. Its proud, long-faced owner met them at the door. He was dressed in clean work overalls and his thin hair stood wilder than she remembered.

"Ms. Andrews, I hadn't realised you were coming so early. And Freya, what a pleasant surprise!"

"The early bird catches the worm, or so I hear," said Ms. Andrews with a tight-lipped smile.

He returned the expression, his long face softening somewhat. "I hadn't reckoned on lovely creatures such as yourselves hankering after worms, now..."

"Perhaps some bacon, then?" The words tumbled quickly from Freya's lips.

He stared into her eyes before replying. His own eyes were small, shrewd, set deep into the hollows of his face. Confronted with the unexpected challenge, she stared boldly back, relishing the unexpected thrill that raced within. It felt curious but not unpleasant; a bristling at the back of her neck, which coursed like blood through her veins, setting light to her nerves with animal fervour. The wind buffeted her face, scented with smoke and cold against the hotness of her skin. After what felt like forever, he spoke again. "Couldn't wait until market on Thursday, my dear? Not that I blame you, mind..."

"We're running low," she said, "the children have quite an appetite lately. I don't know where they put it all."

"I'm sure you don't," he said, still staring quite intently. Then, as though snapping from a dream: "Yes, I think I can stretch to some bacon. Here, come in. Let me take your coat. How about some sausages, too?"

"Why not?" she said, smiling, delirious with unspoken defiance. "Lead the way."

* * *

Despite moving to Lynnwood only nine years ago, John McCready had settled very quickly into the community. He was no stranger to village life, having lived in nearby Ashurst for many years before. The McCreadys had owned land there for centuries and were famously proud of their title as Commoners, which authorised them the care of their own land. The Forest was a law unto itself. They understood that better than most in Lynnwood.

The farm had meant everything to John's family. He had spoken at length with Freya about his childhood there, when first moving to Lynnwood. Mostly she had wondered what drove him from Ashurst, where so many of his roots were based.

"My sister," he said plainly that day, and she had known from the look in his eyes that she would not like what followed. "Mary was an unsettled woman. Even when we were children she would hear things. Noises at her window, or from the sties."

"Noises?"

"The pigs, screaming at night. Sometimes it was the cows. The farm was no place for a young girl."

"We're more resilient than you think," Freya said, smiling. He did not smile back.

"Have you ever heard a cow scream, my dear? Or a pig?"

"I haven't, no."

"Then let us hope you never have to." He took a long draught of his drink before continuing, his lips white with foam. "When my sister didn't get better, they took her to the doctor. Dosed her up on pills. Little tablets, all kinds of colours, to make her social, like. It seemed to work, I suppose, though she was never the same since."

"I'm so sorry, John."

"Happen the part of her that heard those sounds was the good part, the real Mary. The pills put a stop to that, anyway. For a while at least. She grew up right enough, though she was never fit to leave the farm again. Then one day, they stopped working."

"Just like that?"

"Just like that," he said. "I'd only recently moved back to the farm myself. Our father was not long gone and my mother couldn't cope with all the heavy work herself. So I came back, with my brothers, to help look after the place. That was when Mary started playing up again. Hearing things that weren't there. Seeing figures in the morning fog."

"Wasn't there anything you could do?"

"It all happened so quickly. Besides, what could anyone do, when she was struggling to surface? I swear it, the old Mary was trying to break free. It never did sit right with me, when they gave her those pills. Anyway, they said she'd built up some resistance, when they examined her afterwards, but I knew. I knew she was fighting.

"We found her in the stables one morning. Curled up in

the corner, naked, stiff as the table here." He struck the wood with the palm of his hand. "They said the cold got her. They said they were sorry. I didn't know what to believe, but I couldn't stay there anymore. All I could see was that shape in the corner of the stables, so old but so young-looking, and so vulnerable like. And I remembered Lynnwood."

He had visited the village several times, it emerged, during his formative years, and something of Lynnwood had remained with him ever since. She had heard similar stories before and was not surprised. The village had a way of sticking, in the mind and in the soul. So he had sold his shares of the farm and bought the rights to new land, here in the village, and had not looked back since.

* * *

The clearing stood near Mawley Bog, not far from the Hanging Tree. Smaller and more intimate than she had imagined from Ms. Andrews's telling, there was nonetheless room for the pair of them to wander. The old woman walked slowly, as though in her dream, twigs breaking beneath her tread. Sunlight shone down through the branches, which stretched overhead. Even the bark glinted silver with hoar frost, bright against the rotten branches on the ground.

"You see, Joan? No flies, just trees. They're just trees."

Freya's voice shattered the silence; a human voice, so out of place in this copse, this wild place, encased in a layer of cold. Only then did she realise how uneasy she felt. It might have been the stillness of the scene, or the hallowed quiet of the Forest in the absence of bird calls or the trickling brook, their dirges frozen on the air, as water to sheets of ice. And it was quiet. Every hollow snap beneath Ms. Andrews's feet echoed between the trees, until they might have been coming from anywhere in the Forest. The icy air pricked Freya's lungs with each savage breath, emerging again as a pale cloud when she exhaled.

"Lord in Heaven..." muttered Ms. Andrews, her back to Freya. "Oh Lord in Heaven..."

"Joan, what is it?"

"I'd forgotten... God forgive me. Lord! Forgive me for what I've done."

Alone together in the clearing, with only the trees and the cold for company, the enormity of those words crept agonisingly down Freya's spine. And with every word spoken, it seemed as though the trees crawled closer, the branches longer, the cold harsher. Her pulse thundered hot in her temples and it might have been her imagination but she thought she saw something between the trees; a thin figure moving swiftly around the outskirts of the clearing. Her throat tightened, her eyes distracted. The wind took Ms. Andrews's scarf, tossing it to the trees.

"Joan, what had you forgotten? What do you see?"

Another flash of movement, as something continued to circle the glade. She would have followed it except Ms. Andrews turned to her then. Never had she seemed so physically frail, as if drained by the chill air or the forest roots until only the ghost of Ms. Andrews remained. And yet there was a feverish light in her face, shining in her eyes, visible in those vaguely parted lips. Her scrawny frame trembled – from the cold, Ms. Andrews would later confess, as they walked back through the trees.

57

"Joan, I'm so sorry. I didn't realise. I didn't know you had... memories here."

"No flies," said the woman dumbly. "You were right... No flies."

"We should go. I can't apologise enough. Let's get you inside and warm. Have you seen Eaton? I think he ran into the trees."

Hearing the crunch of dead leaves behind her, she turned, to grab the dog, leash him and leave this wild, menacing place. Except the shape that burst from the undergrowth behind her was not Eaton, or any dog. Long, human arms reached for her. Bones clicked as the figure scrabbled closer, face twisted, mouth gaping, eyes fixed feverishly on her own –

This instinct was different. She fell back from the apparition, tumbling into the blanket of leaves. She could not challenge the sheer savagery of that vision, or the fact that behind the ecstasy in its eyes, the hunger that split its lips, it had seemed so familiar.

They hurried from the place; two small silhouettes beneath the vastness of the skies, the trees and the long, hungry howl of a dog.

CHAPTER EIGHT

Though no one confessed it, the residents of Lynnwood sought their missing vicar for their own savage curiosity as much as Ms. Andrews's welfare. When the news broke that she had vanished, they rushed from their homes and the village crawled with insatiable activity; figures moving swiftly, bent low with desperation, through the streets.

Once it was determined she was nowhere in the village borders, one question quivered, unspoken, on everyone's lips, hidden beneath the proper questions they voiced: what had become of Ms. Andrews since surrendering to the wild glamour of the Forest?

Joan Andrews's funeral was a formality. Lost to the trees there was no body to bury. The village gathered in the graveyard behind Allerwood Church where they prayed for their vicar, even as they stood upon the mouldering remains of those hundreds who had died before. Freya had never realised the hypocrisy of it, the sheer madness of such celebrations. Life was spirit, yes, but spirit made flesh; the kiss of the wind against one's face, the rushing of hot blood beneath one's skin, the swelling, irrepressible urges that flooded one's body with every hurried thump of the heart. In death, there were none of these things. Nothing but ethereality, reduced to insubstantial memory, so easy to scatter, no better than a dream, or the orange leaves of a tree in autumn. And then the body, stripped of the self; a cooling collection of limp limbs and ragged flesh, growing soft and syrupy with decay.

She attended the funeral with Catherine, two spectres in a congregation of famished ghosts. Mrs. Morecroft took the sermon. She spoke of Ms. Andrews's childhood in the village, then Frederick, and her role as vicar of Lynnwood. Others took the floor with their own memories, their own private interactions. Each anecdote pricked Freya until she thought she must be pink and flushed with shame. This was her fault. She had led Ms. Andrews to the trees. She had urged the old woman through the Forest, where she wouldn't have stepped alone. She had forced her into that place, which was so far from the village, and it had swallowed her whole with a verdant, vacuous roar...

She clung to the tears, hot and wet against her skin. Something had happened that morning in the Forest that she had not expected. The hunger had grown too great, too wild, bursting from every vein beneath her skin until she thought she might lose herself. Surrendering to her appetites whenever she felt them, she had not dwelt on how dangerous they were, or why they were repressed in the first place. She had thought them delightful, then wildly indulgent, but never deadly.

They must be reined in, she vowed. The feasting, her visits to the brook, these things must be stopped before they consumed her. Already, it seemed, they had nipped at her flesh, stealing bite after bite, and then in the clearing with Ms. Andrews, a monstrous mouthful, pale-faced and ghastly in the undergrowth.

She endured the rest of the ceremony in silence. Though there were no remains and, therefore, no grave, a traditional headstone was nonetheless erected. Once this had been appreciated and the ceremony concluded,

Lynnwood's residents broke away, one by one drifting back into the village. As the last to leave, her face red, fingers pink from the cold, she was the only witness to Mr. Shepherd, the village artisan, and the gift he dropped quickly onto the headstone before himself departing.

Close inspection revealed it to be a brooch. Though ornate in design, it was hammered from little more than iron. She touched it tentatively. No bigger than the palm of her hand it proved smooth to the skin and icy cold, as if devouring the warmth from all around it. But more than the cold or the intricacy of the brooch, the depiction she saw in it struck her, causing a sharp inhalation of breath; the brooch resembled an open mouth, distended and ravenous, gaping up at her from the metalwork.

CHAPTER NINE

Freya thought often of the moment in which McCready's gaze had met with hers that day outside his farmhouse; the second when, challenged by his eyes, carnal instinct had bubbled to the surface. Civility decreed she fled; it taught to run from conflict, or to console it where possible, to neuter it as a dog relieved of its potency. But she had stared into McCready's eyes, bright with understanding, and recognised the hunger. She held his gaze unflinching, even as her lips formed the lies she had known they would. And though she concealed the truth, there was no hiding the lustre in her own eyes, as she had seen in his.

The memory served as a constant reminder of what lay beneath the skin, waiting to escape, should she let her guard down for but a moment. For weeks afterwards she clung to the commonplace, becoming a regular face about the village, where before she would have walked Eaton through the trees. The routine of Sunday service was unsettled but she didn't let this deter her from the church grounds. And if she thought there were more headstones of late, more graves than she could ever remember seeing, this could surely only be a good sign; the village becoming clearer and more solid around her, grounding her in the real, the now?

Her dream too began to change, as though subject to the turning seasons. The trees shed their leaves, branches seemed to twist and the dulcet song of the water fell silent beneath sheets of opaque ice. Winter had come to the dream-brook, and each time she glimpsed the thirsty figure opposite, with its hands dipped into the chill waters, it seemed thinner and less-kindly, until she began to doubt its motives by the pleasant brook, and dreaded the moment their eyes, for that one second, met.

* * *

The Knightwood Oak, two miles walk from the village across heathland, stood for all that was ancient and enduring about the Forest. From where Freya waited with her daughter beside the small picket fence that surrounded the monstrous tree, the sanctity of the scene could not have been more apparent; the enormity of the wild, maternal edifice, reaching into the sky as it had done for hundreds of years, surrounded by a court of saplings; its children, cut from its own flesh and blood.

Even this mighty tree was not exempt from man's influence. Men dressed the practice up as pollarding, they validated their actions with reason, but this did not detract from the violence of their axes as they stripped back branches and brought the tree low for another hundred years. As though the tree would not have endured, not procreated, without their 'help', their 'encouragement'.

In that moment, staring up into the branches, she felt ashamed to be human. If it was the beasts who lived alongside the tree, who nested in its branches and hunted in its shadow, then let her be a beast, not the other; desperate to rise above the wilderness so inherent to man's heart. She could see that now.

Stepping closer, Freya took her daughter's hand in her own. Lizzie looked frail, as though the breath of wind that touched her hair might blow a little stronger and take the rest of her away with it. Freya hoped that she was happy. It had been so long since they had spoken properly, never mind laughed, or baked together, or played as they had used to, when Lizzie was little.

* * *

The blue light of winter shone through the kitchen windows, revealing an uncluttered room, sparsely filled, save for ingredients massed in one corner of the worktop. A calendar hung from the wall, beside the AGA cooker, marking December in all its festive glory. The year was 2004, though it could have been any winter's day; barely the afternoon, darkness already encroached on the village. A string of fairy lights hung from the ceiling beams.

"What are we making?" said Lizzie, her face caught in the glow of the lights. "Are we making cakes? Are we making mince pies for Father Christmas?"

Looking down at her daughter, Freya smiled. The girl's cheeks still shone from the cold. They had not long returned from the market, where it had begun to snow. Some of the flakes still lingered in her hair. "It's a bit early for mince pies, darling. We'll make some tomorrow, or the day after, so they'll be fresh when he visits. They taste the best when they're freshly-made."

"What are we making now, then?"

"Bread," said Freya, "using an old family recipe. Your grandmother taught me how to make it when I was a little girl, and her mother before her."

"But bread..."

"Special bread," she said. "It's extra tasty, you'll see. Here, help me weigh out the ingredients. It's important

64

we measure everything just right."

They went through the ingredients one by one, sifting them into bowls and filling measuring jugs. Freya had weighed out everything beforehand; seven grams of yeast, a pinch of salt, fifteen grams of softened butter and one cup and a half of wholemeal flour, but that wasn't the point. It was the process that mattered. The activity.

"What next?" said Lizzie, her hands white, face powdery with flour. Against the redness of her cheeks she resembled a porcelain doll; one of the old-fashioned Victorian types, made up like proper ladies.

"You have to be patient," said Freya, "we're nearly done."

"Why do I have to be patient?"

"Because some things take time, darling."

"I don't think I'll be patient," said Lizzie decisively.

"When?" said Freya.

"When I grow up. It sounds boring."

A controlled burst of water, unleashed for one maddening moment, swirled inside the measuring jug, then Freya set to work. Taking Lizzie's hands in her own they mixed the ingredients together, as another girl had with her own mother, nearly four decades earlier. The gentle sighs of the mixture, as she worked it with her hands, filled the kitchen. The emerging dough felt soft, almost spongy, beneath her fingertips.

Nobody had made bread like Harriet, especially when generously spread with one of the Allwood's jams. The blackberry was always Freya's favourite as a girl. She remembered her mother's cakes, laden with succulent fruits; swollen blackberries, bursting raspberries, sticky and shiny with glaze under the afternoon sun. Though Freya had always been her father's daughter, the hours spent baking with Harriet were instrumental in their bonding. The act of creation, of making something out of nothing, was one close to every girl's heart, no matter her age, especially when those creations were crumbling scones, loaves of springy bread and glazed fruit tarts, sharp and sweet against the tongue; sheer sensuality, real and regenerating.

"Am I doing it right?" said Lizzie.

"You're a natural, darling. Much better than I was, when I was your age."

"Really?"

"Yes!" said Freya. "Maybe you'll become a baker one day. Then you could sell your cakes at market, like we saw today."

From where Lizzie stood, between Freya's arms, she snorted: "I'm not going to be a baker."

"You're not?"

Shaking her head, Lizzie looked up from their hands. Her eyes were sharp, bright, and suddenly there was nothing porcelain about her. "I'm going to be a runner," she said. "I'm going to run through the trees, faster than anyone else, and I'm going to keep running, just like Dad."

Freya's fingers sunk into the dough and remained there a moment. "Your father's run too far," she said. "He's run so far that he's got lost, somewhere in the Forest. Promise me you'll never run that far."

Lizzie promised. "You know, it seems to me a lot of people get lost in the Forest."

They spent the rest of the afternoon preparing the dough. When they finally finished, and Freya withdrew her hands from her daughter's, she noticed a faint red imprint where her wedding ring had pressed into Lizzie's skin. For a whole hour afterwards Lizzie pranced around the house, a dishcloth over her face, humming wedding songs and pretending she was to be married.

Only when the dogs began howling did Freya draw the curtains and usher Lizzie upstairs, mimicking the wolfish sounds as she chased her shrieking daughter into bed.

* * *

The Forest had grown dark this year, intimidating, alive with the movement of dead trees and memories, but when Lizzie had asked to see the Oak, Freya had been only too happy to oblige. She savoured this fleeting moment, in which the beauty of the trees was restored, this abused tree towering over its saplings, mother and daughter beneath it. She would think of it often, in the weeks ahead, when so much else became ugly and unkempt.

Presently they grew cold and hungry. As the afternoon set in and the light began to leave them, they set off for the village across the heathland, where the ponies ran wild as they pleased...

* * *

"I'm worried about Merlot," Catherine said, when Freya visited her old friend that evening for drinks. "She hasn't come home. Not since last night."

The cottage itself was beautiful. Freya had often thought it belonged in a fairy tale. Scarlet ivy crawled across the grey brick outside, stretching around the door to the first-floor windows. The roofing was dark slate that shone a gorgeous black in the rain and warmth suffused the inside of the cottage, so that on cold winter evenings there was nowhere nicer or more welcoming in the village. Beams lined the kitchen ceiling, from where wicked witches would hang their cauldrons. Catherine had opted for spice baskets and begonias. The room filled with the oaky scent of red.

"Spill the beans," Freya said, when her friend risked yet another glance at the window. Catherine's distress was palpable.

"What do you mean?" said Catherine.

"I haven't seen you this anxious since your father caught us swigging that expensive fizz the afternoon we finally finished school."

"That night..." Catherine smiled, her eyes flickering to Freya's. "I thought we were never to speak of that night again. We swore, remember?"

"We're not," said Freya, smiling back. "We're speaking of tonight."

They moved with their wine into the sitting room. Freya poured fresh glasses while Catherine sorted them some finger-food. It was cosier here, nestled into the sofas. The air was laced with languor. Freya took a sip of her wine, relishing the full-bodied taste of it, the feel of it slipping down her throat, while Catherine voiced her concerns.

Merlot was Catherine's cat, one of three, named after her favourite French grape. The animals meant a great deal to the woman, who treated them like her babies in the absence of children of her own.

"I'm sure she can look after herself," Freya said. "Isn't that the point of cats?"

"The point of cats..." Catherine rolled her eyes. "That's hardly fair. I don't quiz you on the point of dogs, do I?"

Freya laughed with genuine mirth. "I'm not sure dogs have a point, unless you count eating and trailing mud through the house, and I can hardly criticise him for that lately."

"You old bitch," said Catherine, laughing with her now. "What a pair we make."

"To Merlot," said Freya, raising her glass.

"To Merlot!"

They talked long into the night, Catherine's worries drowned beneath a cocktail of wine and memories. Many bottles were drunk, until there was no more Merlot of any sort in the cottage and Freya was forced to return home, before she lost the ability to walk. Retreating quietly from the cottage, she left Catherine where she had passed out on the sofa.

Only when Freya was outside did she trip, and curse her bra for being so restrictive, and almost fall into a flowerbed. The night seemed to swim around her. The alcohol had gone down well, she thought, as she stumbled home. Though she knew she would suffer tomorrow, she would drink again with Catherine soon. For Merlot's sake, if an excuse was ever needed, which it wasn't, in Lynnwood.

CHAPTER TEN

December settled silently over Lynnwood one night and with it an awareness; the worst kind, not of monsters or evil but the nature of the self, penned between the pages of a diary.

Night emerged from the Forest. It spilled from the dark spaces between the trees as much as the skies, rolling out across the village. There were no carols to commemorate its arrival, no children playing in the streets, no sounds at all, in fact, save for the muffled coughs of lonely silhouettes, bent low as they struggled home. Counted among them, Freya moved swiftly through the night. Her old Parka was zippered to her neck, so that only the tail of her scarf fluttered with the wind.

She should have returned home hours ago. She should have been there to meet George and Lizzie after school, to gather them up and lock the doors and comfort them. Instead she had remained at the Vicarage, poring over the books that Ms. Andrews had so diligently guarded all these years. Once she had begun, once she had deciphered the antiquated English with its wild scrawl and long-limbed lettering, she couldn't seem to stop until she reached the last page of each volume and felt the maddening truth of their echoes...

* * *

They raised the issue of the Vicarage three days before, while meeting in the village hall. Fewer than were expected attended the gathering but then the morning frost had been especially black, the air savage to breathe.

70

Mr. Shepherd was a notable absentee, though McCready's sandwiches more than compensated for the matter, and Catherine arrived a little later with hot flasks of mulled wine to pass around. Gathered together beneath the exposed timber beams of the village hall, they ate and drank these offerings with abandon.

"There's always been an Andrews in Lynnwood to take care of matters such as this," said Mrs. Morecroft, when they had consumed their fill and drank much more. "As we all know, life had other plans for our vicar, God rest her soul, and we aren't afforded this luxury."

"We could hold an auction?" suggested McCready. "Happen we'd make a pretty penny, selling off some of the older items. Village heirlooms and such."

"That only raises more questions," said Mrs. Morecroft. "Which of the Vicarage's treasures were hers to sell, and which belong still to our church? There's local heritage to consider. Then, supposing we make sales, where does the money go? She left no will, no inheritors."

"The village," said someone else. "We could turn it back into the village. Get some decent roads down –"

"Roads! Through-traffic's the last thing we need –"

"We can't sell," said Catherine, blowing wisps of steam from an unscrewed flask on the table. Her eyes, filled with wisdom and wine, wavered through the heat. "These were Joan's things. This was her life. Have some respect for the woman."

They fell silent at these words, each afraid, as if they might have revealed too much of themselves in the presence of their neighbours. With some visible effort, Mrs. Morecroft roused herself to speak further. "This still leaves us with the question of what is to become of the Vicarage."

"We should clear it of her things," said Freya. She hadn't spoken yet, content to listen as the meeting unfolded, but she found herself talking then. The words moved through her mind like a swarm of tiny gnats, dancing above the surface of Mawley Bog in the ragged red of autumn dusk. "Give them away. The Vicarage's not her home anymore, and it's what she would've wanted."

"You're sure, Freya?"

"Yes, I think so. We spoke often enough. I knew her better than most, in the end."

Tension gripped the men and women of the village hall. Freya remembered the tightness of her bra against her flesh, the night outside Catherine's cottage. The feeling extended to the rest of her clothes; a second cotton-skin she sought to shed, revealing the real underneath. She knew the mounting urge to run, break free; to drop low, like dogs or ancient man, and race from Lynnwood into the half-light of the trees, as they imagined Joan Andrews to have done, and she knew she was not alone in feeling this. Some of the villagers, she would later learn, dreamt they had seen the old woman in the woods since; a wiry figure, naked and shrivelled, scrabbling through the trees.

The tension about the room grew tighter until she thought it might shatter like a stressed branch and splinter into a hundred pieces. Somehow, Mrs. Morecroft spoke. They voted in favour of clearing the Vicarage. Freya chose to tackle the study and the literature housed within.

* * *

She fled through the village. The night pressed down on her, a numbing blanket. She found relief in that numbness; a deadening of spirit and body, as though she drifted through the streets, born by the wind and nothing more. The sound of her boots as they knocked against the cobbled streets formed a frantic rhythm into which she was absorbed.

She should never have delved into the diary. But it had lain open on Ms. Andrews's desk, in that tired study filled with the accumulated dirt of ages. Crisp white pages had caught her attention, offset by the wide, frantic scratches of black ink across them, where so much else was dark and dusty with abandonment. The room itself looked as though it had not been used properly for many years, save certain marks, made recently in the dust. She followed these tracks, the lingering echoes of Ms. Andrews's last movements, and had found the diary, so innocuous as to be monstrous given the truths of which it spoke. Even as she had read it, curious at first, then with wide eyes and quivering lips, she knew them to be just that; truths, written and forgotten but remembered with the coming of the cold and the snow and Winter Solstice...

* * *

Taking the diary from where it lay on the desk, she turned the book over in her hands. The cover bore no name. Nor did its pages contain any obvious dates. Indeed, no effort of time-keeping had been made, as though that was unimportant. She leafed through the leather booklet slowly. Where the ink was older and more faded she discerned the earliest entries, but it was the most recent additions, in that long, hurried lettering, which were of interest to her. She read steadily at first, then with increasing quickness, as one who has glimpsed the horror of something and is thereafter unable to look away, both enthralled and afraid that they might miss something, or that the same horror should be worse only half-known.

Joan had written of her dreams; the clearing, the dusk, the fly-faced woman through the trees. Something about reading these visitations made them more real, certified by shaking hand and scratchy ink; the dreaming thoughts of a frightened woman, committed to paper. She wrote of other things too; the encroaching cold, the sounds of the Vicarage, the yellowing of the leaves of the alder trees by the church. Freya deduced from these things that it was October, though they were fleeting mentions. Always, it seemed, Joan returned to the dreams, as they returned to her each evening, when the sun fell and shadows filled her home.

Trepidation crept into the writing, or sleeplessness, characterised in the fragility of the lettering, the frantic pace at which it rushed across the pages. The trees, she wrote, seemed taller, the dusk dimmer, the fly-faced woman closer. There was night after night of this; each marked by a sole step across the deadwood through the dappled gloom. On reading these things, Freya grew quite sad. The feeling was physical; sickening in her stomach, mixed with pangs of regret. Who was she, to have suggested that walk through the Forest? So naïve to assume that it could heal, that it could help. She, who covered herself in clothes, who could not even bear to look at herself in the bathroom mirror, for fear of what she might see in the steamy glass?

Then came the inevitable entry, which she had been both dreading and eager to read. "Tonight we met halfway across the clearing, under the branches of the alders. I reached out and stroked the woman's arm. There are few words to describe how lovely and horrid it felt, to feel her flesh against my fingers, so warm and familiar. Her human parts were smooth, and pale as milk in the fading light. I did not touch her face, not because I feared it by this point, but because there was no need. I have realised why I have been dreaming of her, and she is not a thing to fear. Instead I brought my hand to my own face, running it across my cheeks, my skin, the curvature of my head, and found it to be that of the fly. We are one and the same, this figure and I. She is me. I am the fly-faced woman, and I have remembered why I stand in that Gadarene clearing, night on night, alone and bearing the face of the Lord of the Flies, the Gluttonous One, the Prince of Hell...

"On touching my face and confirming these things, I found myself alone in the Forest. Either I had become the figure, or she had never been. One and the same, I fled from that place, overcome with a burgeoning sense of fear. The trees reached out for me as I broke through the brush. Leaves caught in my hair – I had hair, now, and my own face again – and breath blew in white clouds from my mouth. The sun had died and everything seemed frozen. And though I fled aimlessly, there were sounds ahead, growing closer and closer, not approaching me, but I towards them, and I realised – no, I remembered – I was chasing him through the trees, I was chasing him, I was chasing him, and then I felt it inside..."

The writing grew nearly illegible. Ink had seeped into the page and become faint, where wetness had made it run. Freya's throat felt dry, her lips cracked, her eyes narrow as she strove to read on. There was more scripture, and much talk of flies and demons, and then, on the last page, a confession:

"Only the Forest matters now. Heaven must wait its turn, if He will forgive me my actions. Have I done wrong by Frederick? Have I sinned, by chasing him through the trees that night and sating myself on him, by gorging myself on his flesh, his blood? My God, I can barely write the words, yet even as I do so my stomach grows impatient, my mouth wet with saliva. It is an abhorrent and monstrous thing I have done, in the throes of a hunger that was not my own, and entirely my own. I feared I was a Beast, and that Hell awaited me. Then I realised this was not the case, or that we are all beasts underneath. There is no devilry in what I have done. Do foxes not pick at their prey? Do dogs and cats not eat flesh where they find it? He must forgive me, for I have acted only according to my nature, as it is all things' nature to grow hungry and hunt.

"God made me in His image, and I am ravenous, as I once was, so many years ago. I must embrace this hunger, before it happens again in such a violent and uncontained fashion. I go to the Forest, where I shall run and be free and perhaps find Him in the trees and the earth, if not in myself."

* * *

At every turn Freya saw the terrible things of which she had read. Shadows formed silhouettes locked in ravenous embrace. The wind added sound to their feeding forms, Frederick Mangel's screams carrying through the years as his famished fiancée tore into him. And all the while Freya's boots knocked against the cobbles, matching the hurried pace of her heart, which raced, terrified and exhilarated, in her chest.

She saw the village differently now. Lynnwood had transformed in her eyes, reduced by ink and night into formless shapes; a meaningless collection of bricks and stone in the vast sprawl of ancient, untamed forest. Their ancestors heard the bellows of the Forest's breaths, the thrumming of the trees, the groaning of the earth beneath their feet, and in their horror they built houses and streets and a small church, anything to distance themselves from the roaring hunger of the trees, which so echoed the stirrings inside each of them. Each Midwinter families were found, broken apart across their sitting rooms. Husbands plastered bloodily to their armchairs. Wives in pieces down the landing. And both devoured; great strips torn from their backs, limbs and breasts removed, as though they were livestock and nothing more, like the pigs kept by McCready. Some years only the bones were left, sobering and sick in the cold light of morning, the occupants of Lynnwood, reduced to their grinning, fleshless cores.

Joan's diary was but one in a study filled with confessions. Lynnwood had been built on a legacy of hunger, as far back as those earliest settlers. Though the forest soil was poor, there was little people would not do, or eat, when it meant the difference between life and death. Even in the winter months, when darkness dragged and bodies froze, there was meat to be found, if they would only eat it. There, perhaps, she had found the roots of Lynnwood's legacy; the earliest records of that nameless hunger, between the starving hollows of the trees.

And though the village had become a pleasant enough place in which to live, these hardships forgotten, their hunger had survived, carried in the blood and beneath the skin.

CHAPTER ELEVEN

Hear the music of the brook
Running through the trees,
Over pebbles, under stones,
Wherever it may please.

Smell the turning of the leaves,
Rich autumn in the bark,
The season sings a merry song
Its voice that of the lark.

See the water run its course,
The Forest, now awoken,
River shining in the light
And at its banks, the Bauchan.

He makes a very pleasant sight,
His long face pale and glowing
Of his hunger deep beneath
Why, none of it is showing!

His sopping lips spread wide apart
From them a pleasant song
He beckons so delightfully
Why, he could do no wrong!

But should you step onto the bank
Where earth and water meet,
He'll pounce on you, all tooth and bone,
Another treat to eat!

CHAPTER TWELVE

Standing in the window in her front room, as she had each day for a week now since that revealing night, Freya stared out over the street. Upstairs, her children slept. She clutched a tumbler of brandy – an old, thick-cut glass, inherited from her father – from which she took a sharp sip.

Lynnwood was quiet, but not peaceful as it had once been. It would never be peaceful again, tainted by the acts, committed in the dark places beneath the trees. She stood there for what seemed like forever. One by one, the other cottages down the street became dark, as Lynnwood closed its curtains, turned off its lights and became still. It was a ghost village, awaiting the arrival of the hungry dead; the bean sí, as one diary had called them. And in a matter of weeks they would come, as they did every Midwinter; not spirits, not demons but the ravenous people of Lynnwood.

Part of her – a very strong part – wanted the hunger to come. She invited its attentions. Let it take her, she thought, and that would be the end of it, of this two-faced existence. There would be no more pretending, no more forgetting, no more wandering the Forest, wondering why she felt so sick, surrounded by such beauty.

But there were other instincts, as primal and fierce as anything that night inspired. While her children slept upstairs, she could not abandon them. Nor could she bring herself to leave Lynnwood; her existence tied to that of the Forest. The very thought of packing up and driving through the trees brought a soft shiver to the back of her neck, as though on entering the Forest she might lose herself once and for all beneath its boughs, and her children with her.

When the last cottage fell dark she dragged her curtains together. She made her way back through the house, switching off each light as she passed. Night spilled into the hallway, the bathroom, the sitting room. Then she climbed the stairs to the landing. Long, oak boards lined the floor, which groaned beneath her tread. The sounds filled the silent house with their presence.

As each night now, she visited first Lizzie's room, then George's. It was her youngest she most feared for. Light spilled from the hallway across his clothes-strewn carpet as she moved to his bedside. She ran a gentle hand through his hair, compelled to touch him, to certify he was still there.

He turned, murmuring softly in his sleep. He really was just a boy; so small, so thin beneath his covers. She thought he would always be her boy, no matter how he grew up or what he became. And, of course, she would do her best to raise him properly, in the meantime. She refused to believe the inescapability of their hunger. She refused to believe that one day he would be driven to feasting beneath the trees. She refused it, as she refused to believe she herself harboured that evilness.

Their atrocities were monstrous, and yet each year they went forgotten. She thought that it was the human way, to deal with life and the horrors it brought. They had not wanted to remember – could not remember – for their own sakes. To remember would be too great a thing to cope with. It made her wonder what else she had forgotten over the course of her lifetime; memories that could not bear to exist.

The room was still and silent as the rest of the house. She licked her lips and continued to stroke her son's hair. It brought her comfort to see Robert's features in his face. It was his eyes, his mouth. These were the corner-marks of a face; defining features of character, of the person within. At least Robert had escaped this madness. At least somewhere he walked free beneath the night sky, and the stars that he had loved so much. She had thought it strange, once, that a man of faith might admire the stars and the shapes they made in the sky. He explained his God was not in Heaven but in the world around them; the trees, the soil, the constellations in the night. When he saw the stars, he said, he was reminded of nature's reach and its burning beauty. None captured that spirit better than his favourite: Orion, the Hunter.

Warmth flooded her limbs, which seemed heavy with brandy and remembrance. Lying down, she wrapped her son in her arms, closed her eyes and in that heady state of mind slipped from wakefulness into sleep.

* * *

She dreamt horrible things; new dreams that may or may not have been real. Shadows stretched for her son's window from all around; long, black limbs reaching for the glass. There was pale movement in the moonlight as scrawny figures clutched at the thatched straw of the roof, faces white and pained. Then sounds; clicking, like tongues against the hollows of mouths, or the cracking of many-jointed legs, and the foetid stench of unwashed teeth as the shadows swarmed closer, a hungry hive, descending on Haven House –

* * *

She woke suddenly in the darkness of the bedroom. Releasing George, she struggled into a sitting position. She felt cold, damp. Sweat plastered her chest and beneath her arms.

She thought to inspect the time. George's clock sat on the bedside table, but she couldn't see its face in the darkness. Beside it was a radio alarm, with a digital clock, but that appeared to have died. It must have run flat, sometime in the night. Rising carefully she slipped from the bed.

Shadows fled from the movement, the curtain caught a breeze, and for a moment she struggled to differentiate between dream and reality. The window was open, even though she was certain she had locked it. She moved quickly across the room, reached for the window latch and closed it. Wind buffeted the frosted glass, rising like a scream into the night, then was still.

Standing there, she stared out over the village. It was a very different place by night. The road stretched on into the darkness until she couldn't distinguish between the two. That seemed right, somehow. Gardens glittered with frost and everything else was black, as though coated in liquorice. She was reminded strangely of *Charlie and the Chocolate Factory*, which her father used to read her when she was young. All that was missing was the swarm of small, child-like figures, rushing through the darkness –

Another gust of wind, another scream, and her

reflection twisted, unsettled. She put the thought quickly from her mind and was about to turn from the window, from the cold, empty blackness of the world outside, when she saw it. Long, apish arms clutching the window frame. And pressed up against the other side of the glass, as far away as she had been seconds earlier, a face. White, gaunt, like that of an old man, but horribly childish, staring at her through the first-floor window.

* * *

She woke, as before, in George's bed. Outside was the deep blue of dawn, growing gradually paler with the rising sun. Birdsong filled the air. She turned to her son, who was once more in her arms, and kissed his forehead. For the briefest moment, she felt at peace. She clung to the moment, savouring it and the soft waves of relief that lapped inside of her.

Then the feeling passed, replaced by another, more insistent urge. Unwilling to ignore it, to risk anything that might make her appetite grow, she rose from the bed and descended through the cottage into the kitchen.

CHAPTER THIRTEEN

When she noticed the brooch on George's windowsill the next morning, she snatched it from sight and placed it in the pocket of her cardigan. She had been made privy to the darkness in Lynnwood, her eyes had been opened to the truths behind Midwinter, and the brooch seemed all the more horrible for it; a thing of delicate beauty in the shape of indelicate hunger, as though commemorating that night and the gaping mouths that filled it. Theirs was an insatiable society. Fine wines, foie gras, blue cheeses and long pork; they consumed these things without conscience. She supposed it was the natural way. Eaton had shown no remorse when chewing on the magpie, and she had lost count of the number of sparrows deposited by Merlot on Catherine's doorstep.

"Sit down," she told George, when she confronted him that afternoon. He hadn't returned straight home from school and it was almost five o'clock before he finally let himself into the house. She waited for him in the kitchen, her anxious hands knotted in her lap. She heard the door open then quietly close, feeling the air grow cold around her as winter rushed into the house. Moments later, his pale face appeared in the doorway.

"I'm home," he said. It was then she had instructed him to sit. He did as he was told. The placid hum of the refrigerator filled the room.

"George, what's this?"

He stared across the dinner table as she produced the brooch from her pocket. It shone dully in the lamplight, dark and grey against the rich grain of the wood beneath.

"It's a brooch," he said. "I think it's made from iron. It looks like a mouth, with teeth."

"And who does it belong to?"

Still staring, he shrugged his slight shoulders. "It doesn't belong to anybody."

"That's not true, George. I know where it's from and who it belongs to because I've seen it before. Why did you take it from the churchyard?"

"I didn't take it," he said. His eyes rose to meet hers, before falling back to the brooch. They swam dark against his pale face. "That would be stealing and stealing's wrong."

"Yes, stealing is wrong, but so is lying, darling."

"I didn't take it," he repeated. "It was a gift."

"A gift?"

"From my friend," he said. "The man in the tunnel."

Her mind jumped back several weeks, to the first time her son had mentioned the man. She remembered patchwork trees, damp soil, the ripe aroma of autumn, as the Forest softened and grew thin, like a piece of brown, shiny fruit.

"The one you saw in the Forest that day?" she said. After a moment he nodded. "I thought you fell out with him, darling?"

"I did. He scared me. But now we're friends again. I didn't know he'd stolen it."

She swallowed, her throat tight, lips pursed. "George, this man..."

"My friend," he interjected.

She forced a smile. "Do you really think you should be friends with him, if he steals?"

86

He seemed to think about this. The flicker of something, she couldn't tell what, crossed his face. "I'm sure he didn't mean to steal. He's nice to me. I feel better when he's around."

"George, I know things are difficult at the moment. The world doesn't feel like a very friendly place. But it will get better, I promise. In the meantime I need you to be honest with me, and with yourself. I think it's wonderful you have this friend, but you mustn't use him to lie for you, as a way of blaming others –"

"I'm not –"

"I need you to be honest with me –"

"I am –"

Pain flashed behind his eyes. His expression tightened, grew sad, such that she thought he might cry. She spoke quickly. "Can I meet him? Maybe if I asked him nicely, he'd put the brooch back where it belongs and none of this will matter."

"He doesn't speak," he said.

"He doesn't speak?"

"No, he just stares. And grins. Besides, you've already met," he said.

"I have? But when?"

"He visited last night, while you were sleeping."

Another face flashed before her eyes; long and white and filled with simian cunning. Imagined from the features of her son, it was all the more horrible; the predatory, formed from the placid. She drew a short breath. "He visits you at night?"

"Yes," he said, as though it were the most natural thing in the world. "He comes into my bedroom, through the window. How else do you think he left the brooch?"

* * *

It was mid-October when George first found his friend in the tunnel. Even autumn could not rob the Forest of its beauty. The trees aged gracefully, turning a hundred shades of brown and red and egg yolk yellow. Clouds gathered overhead, streaky in the dark blue sky, but rain was not unwelcome. Little egrets took to the swollen waters and earthworms turned in the soil. The village transformed into a vivid collage, one of those few places of quiet refuge, which were so rare.

Alone with his thoughts he marched down the tracks. He worked his way methodically from sleeper to sleeper, blissfully oblivious to their history as children are blissfully oblivious to so much of the world. His favourite trainers – the white pair, with light-up soles – found mud again, and a visible weight lifted from his shoulders. He liked to visit this place after school, he told Freya, when she asked him about that day and what drew him to that place on the outskirts of the Forest.

The grass had parted beneath his trainers, their dewy wetness licking the stains from his footwear with every step. He scanned the undergrowth for signs of his quarry; amphibious skin, yellow eyes, or the pink of earthworm flesh. It was perfect weather for hunting, he knew; the rain this morning had been torrential, an endless patter against the school windows, matching the excited beat inside of him as he watched it from inside.

"The streets, overflowin' with filth..." he mimicked, in a depth of voice still many years away.

88

Climbing the slippery embankment, he followed the tracks. When he was roughly halfway along he sat himself down and began to unpack things from his rucksack. The magpie watched him while he worked, from where it perched on the rotten remains of a tree.

A number of items appeared on the tracks beside him. There was a magnifying glass, two of the Allwood's jam jars – one clean, one still sporting the seeded remnants of preserve – a polythene bag filled with crumbs and, last to be retrieved, his pencil case. He set these things down carefully before proceeding to examine the underside of the metal slats and the surrounding mud. When he thought he might have found something he scrutinised it more closely with the magnifying glass. Mostly he uncovered earthworms, brought to the surface by the rain, or drowning woodlice.

The insects understood him. These weren't people with complex emotions. They didn't lie or hide things from each other and they didn't need fathers or school to raise them properly. They simply were. They existed to eat, to breed and, protected by their hard, chitinous skin, they did it very well. The other children found them disgusting. They threw them at each other, stepped on them in the corridors, shivered and squealed whenever anyone spoke about them. He remembered the case of desiccated butterflies, which Freya had hung on the wall in the sitting room; specimens of Papua New Guinea, a gift from an old family friend. Their faded, dusty wings retained an elegant beauty long after death, even skewered inside a display cabinet.

No, there was nothing wrong with insects. Simple

creatures with natural drives, unencumbered by morality or conscience, they were respected. Admirable, even.

He stayed like this for nearly ten minutes, working his way slowly down the length of tarnished track, pausing to examine his findings. Only when he reached the very end of the track did he hear it; a slow, scraping sound. It was a harmless enough noise and yet something about it snagged his attention. He looked up slowly from the mud, the plants, the crumbling remains of rotten timbers, and found himself standing before a tunnel. It stared back at him, empty and vast and dark from the side of the hill.

He fell quiet as he recalled the entrance; a yawning chasm into the earth, where sunlight never reached. He remembered a smell; the moist, metallic tang of minerals. His face had tingled with unspoken fervour.

Standing before the tunnel he heard the sound again; like skin on stone or the scrape of his trainers against the playground tarmac. Except this time he felt it as much as he heard it; an echo in his blood, rhythmic as the drumming of hooves across heathland. He struggled to express the intensity of the feeling, lacking the language or experience to do so, but Freya guessed these things because she too had felt it, when staring down at the pig in the field that morning. It was the stirring of race memories, of those primal sparks long since suppressed beneath the skin; urges that even George, still wild of soul and untamed by adolescence, was unfamiliar with. She could only guess at the thrill he must have experienced; the terror of the unknown.

Though he could not see into the dark he felt a watchful presence inside; a silhouette, almost distinguished from the surrounding gloom. His heart raced, his blood pumped, his hands shook by his sides, but that same terror held him fast.

He never went inside the tunnel. Even before that day he never ventured into the cold, empty place. Freya had warned him often enough how unstable it was, that 'nobody maintains it, George; not since the station closed down.' He had heeded those warnings, it seemed, and for this at least she felt some pride in her son's judgement, even if his own reasoning stung her eyes with tears. He didn't much fancy a rock to the head, he had said quite unashamedly, not if he could help it. He knew that pain well enough already.

For one moment he stood there, surrounded by the damp air, the cold breath of autumn, the streaks of grey cloud overhead. Then he broke and ran. If he possessed the spirit of the lone hunter then it was also true that, faced with the hollow enormity of the tunnel mouth, his resolve broke. Instinct took over and he fled from that wild place to the village and Haven House.

* * *

In the days that followed Freya visited the tunnel herself. It marked the first time she had wandered from the village since learning its dark nature, but for all her apprehension she needed to witness the place herself. She needed to see what George had seen, to feel something of what he had felt.

Still, the tree line watched her as she drew nearer. Though she need not have crossed its borders to reach the tunnel, she felt too close to the Forest already; a shiver racking her nerves as its ancient breath, icy and deep, stung her face. Sounds filled her ears at her approach; long, drawn-out creaks, of wood put under stress, and the rare crack of ice, which echoed through the Forest. The tracks represented a middle-ground into which she had wandered; a halfway place between the village and the vast, verdant sprawl that surrounded it. Not a dozen miles away in Southampton, men and women would be waking and worrying; about morning traffic on the Itchen Bridge, the clothes they were going to wear, or wanted to buy, the bass drone of the cruise ships as they pulled into the city and regurgitated streams of tourists, hot and rank with their own meagre concerns, while in as many steps she would be swallowed by the boughs, lost to Lynnwood and society forever...

She found the tunnel empty. She stared into its mouth for several minutes, trying to replicate George's experience, but could discern nothing in the darkness; no movement, no sense of watchfulness, save that of the trees, in the corners of her eyes. Both relieved and troubled by the imaginary nature of her son's friend, she turned from the tunnel and headed home, following the path of the tracks into the village.

* * *

As a piece of fruit left too long uneaten, Lynnwood began to darken and turn soft; an apple, its brown flesh seething with movement. Once again McCready was woken by a screaming, which he followed this time to the hen house. The birds rushed madly in the moonlit pen, the cold air alive with frantic clucking. And at the centre of the enclosure, birds swarming around its calves, knelt the skeletal figure of before with that same long grin, a hen hanging limply from each hand. Nor was McCready alone in his night-time visitations. Weaker, or perhaps wilder, the children of Lynnwood stirred restless in their beds and dreamt of pale, hungry faces at their windows. And on abandoning his brooch at Ms. Andrews's graveside, Mr. Shepherd found himself unable to sleep. Night after night he tossed and turned, but rest would not come, his body filled instead with a hunger the likes of which he had never known, or could seem to sate with food.

A cry on his lips, McCready chased the figure from the hen house, which slunk like a fox into the blanket of birds and vanished. He woke the next morning with blood in his teeth, feathers stuck to his hands and a vile, coppery taste no amount of whiskey could remove. If the children complained of nightmares they were humoured, or comforted. Most did not, and though they might have seemed more tired than usual, their eyes brighter, their smiles sharper, their dreams went otherwise unnoticed. Mr. Shepherd, distraught at the absence of his brooch, fell upon his workbench with the ferocity of a feeding dog. He hammered iron strips into roughly-hewn pins, twisted metal in his vice, or held it in fire until it was soft enough to shape with his hot fingers. And each time his creations were the same; lips and teeth and lolling tongues. Mouth after mouth filled his workroom, until he couldn't move from his bench for the hunger he had wrought.

CHAPTER FOURTEEN

Freya returned many times to the study in the Vicarage. How could she not, knowing what was written within? The honesty that she found in those pages, however horrid, was nourishing. Mostly, it seemed to satisfy her hunger, or distract her from it, where it might otherwise have consumed her.

Some diaries, as Ms. Andrews's, were confessional. She read tear-stained accounts of feeding frenzies beneath the trees; residents racing through the Forest, converging like a pack of hounds on their human quarry. She read of panicked breaths, of lingering tastes in the mouth and the winter of '42, when the hunger claimed an entire train as it pulled into the village station. After that year the line fell into disuse. The carriages themselves were dissembled. Melted down. The metal, she read, was shipped off to the front line. It seemed an appropriate use for the blood iron, though the residents wouldn't have known this, to ask them.

Other books were more fanciful, their authors seemingly oblivious, poetry spilling like saliva from their lips. On this day in particular she stumbled on a written account of an old village legend. She found it moving for the memories it instilled; the warm security of her father's lap, his hands around her waist, his clear voice in her ears as he recounted the very same folk tale to a young Freya.

* * *

Once, it was said, when the woods were young and the winters long, there lived a man in Lynnwood. This man had a wife, and together they had two sons, and each year when the autumn came and the trees turned red he filled their pantry with food. The winter months were vicious. Frost froze the earth, the trees fell bare and all but the strongest forest creatures sickened, grew thin and died. There was no fruit, there were no roots to dig, except for graves, and so the man worked hard to save supplies and make their larder large before autumn ran its course.

Then one year when the winter came and the snow and ice alongside it, the man's pantry was bare. His wife shook as she asked him what had happened. "Where is our food?" she said, still trembling from fear and the cold. "Why is the larder empty?"

And the man wept – he was an old man now, for the seasons had turned many times since he had first come to Lynnwood – and he admitted that he had eaten the larder's contents for himself. "This winter above all has been so very cold, and I so very hungry, and I had hunted much before the first snow so I thought there would be enough to last."

But there had not been enough to last. The wife shook her head and cursed that human creature, then grew thin and hard and fell stone dead across the floor. And the husband wept at what he had done.

It was not long before his two sons came, attracted by the sounds of his tears. They saw their mother's figure on the floor and they too wept. They asked their father what had happened.

"I have done a terrible thing in eating our supplies," he said. "Everything that we stockpiled is now gone."

"Then, like our mother, we will starve because of you,"

replied his sons.

He continued to shake his head. "I will find more food. You will not starve like your mother. I will be back for you." And so saying he climbed astride his shivering horse and called his world-weary hound and he set off from Lynnwood in search of food.

It was a pale, shining place beneath the frosty boughs. Ice cracked across the forest. His horse's hooves broke the glassy sheets beneath their tread. But there was no food to be found in the New Forest. Day stretched into night and the old man grew colder but he would not return until he could feed his sons. He had given them his word, after all, and they were his children.

Then, in that last moment, he saw it: a smooth-flanked stag, white as snow, with antlers twisting branchlike from its brow.

And so he kicked his horse's flanks and they gave chase, a cry of exultation on his old lips. They raced through the icy undergrowth: beneath the oak, the birch, the aller. They passed the shards of Mawley Bog and then the Hanging Tree. But no matter how fast his horse ran or how close they grew to the stag, it was always just out of reach.

The tale had changed through the telling, but Freya knew that to be the nature of stories, as it is the nature of winter to be cold, or the human creature to glut. Some claimed the old man's name was Cernunnos of the Wildwood. Others said he went by Herne, the Hunter. Others still say there was no stag at all; that the old man chased himself through the thin, grey trees and that he continues to do so forever more, a wintry spectre with his hound, his horse and his guilt.

CHAPTER FIFTEEN

They felt the change in the air; a subtle shift in the wind and rain that swept through the village. It danced across their skin like the scattered steps of a hundred crawling flies; an interminable itch growing stronger and more irritant with each passing day, until one morning when winter broke and with it the news that three boys had been reported missing.

The village embraced the hunt. Neighbours, not carollers, knocked from door to door and the skies filled with the baying of hounds, a full month before Midwinter, as residents followed their struggling dogs over the heathland. The village resonated with dread feeling, visible in the haunted eyes of the residents, if only they knew what they were seeing.

The boys' names were Andrew Stone, Stewart Foxley and Christopher Savage. The Stones and the Savages were relatively new to the village, having moved here in Freya's lifetime. The Foxleys, by contrast, had lived here for many generations and were an established presence. They were wealthy and owned one of the oldest cottages, near the dairy. A loud, exuberant sort, they frequently hosted parties no less loud or exuberant, though Freya had never been invited to one herself. She had Catherine for those kinds of evenings.

The boys had gone missing on Thursday afternoon. Mr. Sandford's son said he saw them walking down the high street, after school. Catherine, shopping in the village for spices, confirmed this. Mrs. Morecroft had been emptying the upper corridor of the Vicarage of Ms. Andrews's belongings, although she didn't notice them pass outside. It appeared they had turned off somewhere along the high street, through the fields that stretched behind it and crossed over into the Forest.

In the days that followed, Freya's motherly concern reached new depths. If three boys from George's school could go missing in the middle of the afternoon, who was to say the same could not happen to her son? She grew hot with anxiety, unspoken fears burning in her blood and pressing at her skin. She couldn't sleep but was woken each night, and found the tension infinitely worse in the darkness. The walls of her bedroom, the borders of the Forest and the night sky were all canvases against which she painted her worries; Boschian landscapes filled with skeletal figures she knew but could not name, and children, fleeing from them, from the vast blackness of the woods. Nor were these dreams but waking thoughts. Lynnwood seemed taut; as though every scrape of the branches from the ash tree outside her window might snap the tension and bring the Forest crashing down around her bed.

But it did not come. The branches continued to scratch the glass. Each night the tension pulled tighter, echoing the knot in her stomach. There was no relief, no matter how chaotic it would have been. In many ways, she thought, this was worse. She turned to Prozac, not to help her sleep – it was no good for that – but to deal with the places her mind began wandering. She had more than enough of the tablets left over from the months following Robert's absence.

She helped in the hunt for the boys, finding herself in

99

the Forest, where she had sworn not to walk again. How could she not help, a mother herself? Everywhere she hoped to see the three boys, huddled and cold inside a dead tree, tucked into a hollow, or beneath the splayed roots of the felled oak by the bog. They were in none of these places. She doubted they were still of this world, swallowed by the Forest, like so many beforehand.

She had read much folklore in the Vicarage. Stories had existed for hundreds of years, purporting the presence of figures in the Forest; otherworldly creatures, slender and fickle, which made their home beneath mounds of earth or inside fungal elf rings. Superstition said they snatched children who wandered into the Forest unaware; her Bauchan of the trees and the earth.

She knew such creatures were fancy. There were no spirits, no demons, only people with famished features and the insatiable cold. Still she scoured the Forest. In her wakening world, of half-chewed magpies and enduring frost and long, sleepless nights, it was all she could do.

* * *

In light of the missing boys, Lynnwood became a different place. It wasn't an obvious change – there was nothing wrong with the village in any physical sense – but it felt different. Frost lingered longer on the ground in the mornings. The birds in the trees seemed quieter, as if they too sensed that something was subtly amiss. Trees, which she passed every day, looked taller and thinner; the Forest's bones picked clean by the season. The village transformed into a harsh, pointed place, full of sharp edges and sheer surfaces; the starving shadow of the

Lynnwood she knew. And there were so many shadows, as though the shade beneath the trees had grown too great and was spilling out, encroaching ever closer on the unsettled soul of their village.

CHAPTER SIXTEEN

The mystery of George's friend in the tunnel didn't stop with his fleeing from the vast magnitude of the opening that morning.

Amid the pangs of the starving season, Freya remembered other traditions: the devotion to family, to friends, good food and good company. Afraid for her son and his detachment from the village she spent as much time as she could with him. They watched films together; festive and fantastic and ringing with Christmas spirit. They took Eaton for long walks, touring Lynnwood's cobbled streets, illuminated with strings of tasteful lights. And she cooked him hearty meals, the likes of which every growing boy needed; dripping meats, crisp, golden skins, thick gravies and sweet sauces, all washed down with carbonated drinks, which sparkled sharp and refreshing in his face and down his throat. After these meals, when she was briefly sated, her mouth coated with the lingering glaze of dinner, she would sit with him and talk. They spoke of many things, which he might not otherwise have disclosed to her. And while some of these things saddened her, or made her hot and anxious, she wasn't upset because through speaking they grew closer.

He still returned to the old Brockenhurst line each afternoon. They often talked about the place, which seemed so special to him. The tunnel frightened him, as the dark frightened all children, but there was a part of him that recognised the darkness and was excited by it.

* * *

One late October afternoon, while visiting the tracks, George had heard shouts behind him. The unwelcome voices startled him, his heart racing in his chest. Still on his hands and knees, where he had been inspecting the sleepers for beetles, he looked around. Three boys were moving towards him from the trees.

"What the hell?" said the closest. He thought it might have been Andy.

"What's he doing up there?"

"He's playing with dirt –"

"No, worms! He's eating worms!"

He lost track of who was speaking because he had turned back around to pack away his things, and then it didn't matter because they started to chant, their ugly voices joined in childish ritual. They reached him just as he was refilling his rucksack. Chris snatched the bag from beneath him while Andy interposed himself between the two. Stewart took the bag from Chris and emptied it onto the grass. His equipment tumbled out.

"So this is where you go after school every day," said Andy.

"You said we should follow him," added Chris. "Look at all this stuff."

"Looks like shit to me." Stewart picked up the polythene bag and emptied the crumbs across the ground. He retrieved one of the jam jars – the clean one – and stared at him through the glass. It did strange things to his eye, making it appear larger than it actually was, multifaceted and sharp. "What d'you use this stuff for?"

When he didn't speak, Stewart hurled the jar against the tracks. The glass shattered against the metal so that only the jagged base remained. "I said what do you use this stuff for?"

Still he didn't answer. His mouth felt dry, powdery, like the wings of those butterflies in the display cabinet at home. This was his place. His private place. And the others had followed him here.

"You're an idiot, Georgie," said Stewart flatly. "Can't speak to save your life, eh?"

"Mouth full of worms, probably," said Chris.

"Mouth full of shit more like."

They taunted him like this for some minutes. He stopped listening after the first, retreating into himself. He wished he were an insect, with glistening black skin hard enough to withstand their words, three pairs of legs, sharp mandibles with which to nip the limbs neatly from the other children, until they were armless, legless stumps, flailing, moaning by the old tracks –

He wasn't sure which one of them pushed him over. He slipped and rolled down the embankment, only stopping when he reached the base. Mud streaked down his back and across his face. His belongings followed after him: some schoolbooks, the second jam jar, his pencil case. His neck ached, his chest constricted. He didn't cry.

"See you tomorrow, Georgie," shouted Stewart. "Don't be late."

He struggled to his feet in time to see Michael hurl his magnifying glass into the tunnel. Then the three of them ran off through the trees.

For a long time he didn't move. A fresh wind played through the orange leaves. Autumn was in full sway, the Forest appearing rich, almost golden, beneath the drab sky, but he saw through that. His was a different Lynnwood, far removed from the village other people seemed to see. Of that much he assured Freya, when they spoke about it.

Eventually he moved, climbing the embankment to the tracks. He found his rucksack and some of his books, which he carefully retrieved from the grass, and was about to leave when he heard it again, as he had before: a scraping sound, of something being dragged against loose rock. He turned to the mouth of the tunnel. The darkness made it near impossible to see and yet he thought he could discern something within: a shape, gaunt and grey in the shadows.

He leant in, his eyes squinting, just as it emerged from the tunnel mouth. Not all of it, but an arm, long and thin. The limb stretched out from the darkness, hurled something through the air, then withdrew in a flash. George stared down at the grass by his feet and at his magnifying glass, lens cracked, which had landed there.

He approached the tunnel slowly. It was darker than he remembered. Colder. It towered over him. There was no more movement, no sign of anything within, except the distant echo of dislodged stones. He stared a moment longer, then spared a backwards glance to make sure he was unwatched. Only the magpie witnessed his actions.

He turned back to the tunnel. His pockets bulged with the collected detritus of the afternoon's efforts: a handful of dead woodlice, a shrivelled earthworm, caught above ground for too long, a small Tupperware box that he had placed two large snails inside. Each of these things he took slowly from his pockets and arranged on the ground

105

before the tunnel. He wasn't so close that the figure inside could reach him; of that he was certain. Friendship was still a strange thing, whatever form it took, and he treated it accordingly.

Seated on the ground, surrounded by his menagerie of insects, living and dead, he opened his mouth and began to talk. He talked about arthropods and habitats and how lonely he felt in a village where no one understood him. He spoke of other things too; the beating inside him, a soft, insistent pulsing, like a pupa pressing at its cocoon.

It didn't matter that the figure in the cave remained anonymous. In fact, he thought, it was better that way. He talked to it, the figure who had watched him when he came to the tracks each day, the figure who had returned his magnifying glass to him. He talked and, though he didn't smile, he was happy because he heard the scattering of tiny stones and he knew it was listening. There were other sounds too; sometimes the sharp, hollow crack of distressed bone, as when Eaton gnawed a chew-treat, and he realised it must be feeding in there, or had fed recently. This didn't bother him unduly, he told Freya, for all things must eat, and he wasn't so alone in Lynnwood anymore.

CHAPTER SEVENTEEN

The brooch's artistic merit was undeniable and Freya was certain it would have stood out among Mr. Shepherd's other wares: the crosses, shield-emblems and burnished crow-shaped pendants displayed each week at market. He was a true craftsman, renowned throughout the village for his Celtic-themed work. She had once commissioned him to make their wedding rings: modest gold bands each sporting a single diamond.

But she had glimpsed the hungry horror inside them all and instead felt only revulsion for the beautiful object in her pocket, which seemed intent on nurturing that nascent wildness. So she sought to return the borrowed brooch to its rightful owner, because it was both the right thing to do and because she wouldn't have it in her house a moment longer.

Stepping out into the village that day, she found the sky white, an uninterrupted stretch of snowy cloud. The village seemed greyer by comparison, a collection of low buildings with dim windows, roofed with dowdy straw. The trees, which surrounded Lynnwood on all sides, had never looked so dense, so dark. And below the blanket of clouds, plumes of smoke, rising from behind the Old Barn...

She hurried down the street in the direction of the Forge. The title was fitting, given the converted cottage's original function. John Shepherd's family, he could often be heard to claim over a pint at the Hollybush, had lived in the cottage for several generations. The parish records confirmed as much, when curiosity led her to inspect the village documents one day: there had always been a metalsmith at the Forge. She still doubted the true ancestry of the Shepherds, knowing what she did about the nature of family names, but that didn't detract from John's claim to the cottage, or the skill of his hand when he turned it to his craft.

She moved through the village, her boots knocking against the icy cobbles. Lizzie was working on her art at a friend's house, so she had asked Catherine to watch George for the afternoon. Catherine had looked after both of her children many times during their infancy. When Lizzie was first born she had made Catherine godmother; the result of a schoolgirl pact beneath the ash tree in her garden.

* * *

The smell of blossom and motor oil filled the garden. It was the first day of spring. The afternoon growled with sound as Freya's father dragged his lawnmower back and forth, reducing the grass to short, bristly clumps, chewed and spat in the machine's wake. Freya thought the lawn looked worse afterwards, but then grass never grew well in Lynnwood. Her father had explained it to her once; something to do with the Forest roots absorbing all the nutrients, leaving none for the lesser plants. She hadn't wholly understood, at the time.

Catherine and she sat beneath the ash tree as dusk descended. They had been sitting there since school finished for the day and were both still dressed in their uniforms. The year was '78 and they were eleven. They should have long outgrown fairy tales and fancy dreams,

108

though neither of them seemed to have realised this. Having mown the lawn, David returned inside. The girls busied themselves with plucking the yellow grass from the soil.

They swore many things that day. Always to play. To laugh. To live together in Haven House with their dogs and their cats and the sounds of the Forest through the open cottage windows. When Catherine realised they might one day have to marry boys she grew sad, then excited, then thrilled at the prospect of motherhood in the way only young girls could.

"I'm going to have two babies!" she said.

"I'm going to have three!"

Catherine scrunched up her face at Freya's declaration. "You can't have three, there's not enough room in the house."

"I'll have as many babies as I want, thank you very much. And you'll have to help me look after them."

"I don't think so," said Catherine. "I mean, it's a lovely thought, but I'll be far too busy with my own to look after yours. And you'll have a husband for that, anyway."

"I still want you to be there," said Freya coyly. Her cheeks grew hot and she plucked a little faster at the grass.

"I suppose I could be their godmother, if you really wanted."

"Yes!" said Freya. "I mean, I'd like that very much."

At that tender age, words still seemed fleeting. Freya remembered the sharp, sudden pain as she pricked her thumb on a piece of bark from the tree behind her, and the splash of red that had fallen from her thumb to the soil below. The bare earth around the tree grew wet with sisterly blood.

It wasn't until her thirties that Catherine learned she was infertile; that she always had been, and would never have children of her own. They were sitting in the same garden when she broke the news to Freya. Merlot of both kinds – cat and grape – had swiftly followed.

* * *

Though Catherine was godmother to both Freya's children, it was George with whom she got on better. Far removed from the shrill, wine-toting woman Freya had grown up with, Catherine was patient and accommodating with her son. When Freya and Robert used to return home from dinner, on those occasions when they treated themselves to meals out, they would often be greeted by the sleeping pair in the front room. Catherine's strong arms would be wrapped around George, his eyes closed, legs dangling from the sofa, or either side of her knee. Asked about this friendship one day, if it could be called such, George had said simply that Catherine was nice, and that she listened when he spoke.

Freya encountered few people along the way to the Forge. Most, she knew, were still scouring the Forest for the missing schoolboys. It might have reflected well on the village that they had rushed so quickly into the dark places beneath the trees. Once, she could remember, not so long ago, she thought men feared those dark places, or the dogs that raced alongside them through the thickets. Now she knew it ran deeper than that, deeper even than blood memories. If they feared these things at all, it was because they craved them; the darkness, in which to hide and hunt, one part of a bestial pack...

They couldn't speak of it, of course. Speech was a different construct; civil and societal. There were no words to express this ancient exuberance or the primal rush of blood and heat and beating heart that accompanied it. Still the village searched, as Freya had searched until she could go no further for fear of losing herself in the gaps between those haunted trees...

Turning down a gravel path, with a little gate and a low brick wall, she watched as the converted cottage emerged from behind the trees. The yard at the front was white with frost and wild snowdrops. Dark windows with lattice bars lined the ground floor of the cottage and, though the first floor was mostly brick, she remembered from previous visits a small window on the other side, above the workshop. Just to the right of the door emerged a weathered pole, from which hung the smithy's sign of old. It creaked painfully on her approach.

For several minutes she waited patiently, her knocking at the door unanswered. She might have waited longer, too, except that the ornament in her pocket seemed to grow heavier, hungrier, as though sensing its return to the one who had made it. Besides, she knew Mr. Shepherd was at home. By all accounts, he hadn't been seen about the village for over a week now.

Even as she moved back from the doorstep and around to his workshop, consternation gnawed at her. She began to fill with dread. Mr. Shepherd was known to lock himself away, sometimes for several days if working hard at his bench, but to miss the village market, and so close to

Christmas, was most unusual. Never mind the search for the missing children, which should have taken priority over anything he was working on.

She moved to the back of the Forge. The gravel crunched beneath her feet. The yard continued around the house, leading to a garden. Though stripped by winter there was still some vegetation to be found; nettles clung stubbornly to life and snowdrops seemed to be flourishing, a bed of pristine petals on delicate green stalks. And behind the garden, joining the side of the house, sat the workshop.

She saw these things in a second. Then she noticed the mouths and her stomach clenched fiercely. Some hung from bird houses; pendants on thin, silvery chains, the shining slip of their tongues extending past their lips. Others were larger; iron emblems hammered into the dusty stone of the residence, teeth like animals' fangs. Still more covered the entrances to those bird houses or littered the leafless bushes and these, she realised with growing horror, were not ornaments but cunning traps; open jaws, spring-loaded and sharp with cruel lips and iron teeth strong enough to break birds or small animals –

Her throat had grown tight, her breaths short, her head light. She noticed strange details in those lasting moments; the grain of the wood used to make the bird houses, hammered and sawed and nailed into a thing of artifice. The aroma of the garden filled her nostrils, fresh and crisp, almost as though she could smell the coldness on the air. She saw the rust-brown stains along the metal teeth of the traps, heard the imagined crash of their jaws as they snapped shut with brutal force –

Then she saw the figure in the window of the workshop. It leant in close, palms pressed outwards, breath steaming the inside of the glass. She had no doubt it was Mr. Shepherd and yet its face was covered by a mask, beaten into the beautiful shape of a beast. Ridges of iron framed its eyes. Ears jutted from either side of the temple, pointed like those of a hound, and its mouth was locked in a horrid howl, which put the meagre brooch in her pocket to shame. The shape of that mouth would not leave her for many days, or the shape of the real mouth beneath, Mr. Shepherd's lips echoing that voiceless howl.

For almost a minute she stared unmoving at the figure in the window, which still pressed, poised, against the glass. Then quite suddenly it lunged, vanishing from visibility like a dog that had grown anxious waiting for its owner to return home, and Freya fled from the garden of mouths. She didn't stop running until she reached the village proper and even then she hurried straight home, not once turning back, not daring, in case that monstrous, magnificent mask dogged her steps, and the man beneath it.

Only once she was safely indoors and tentatively drinking tea did she realise the brooch had fallen from her pocket somewhere when running. Too frightened to be happy, or care that it was lost, she could do nothing but place her lips against the smooth china cup and drink.

CHAPTER EIGHTEEN

The diaries in the Vicarage were more than just informative. Like speech they represented a higher form of communication; structured language, however fragile, amid the hot, chaotic flush of bestial urges. They couldn't hope to tame the hunger that filled Lynnwood; that much was obvious from the volume of literature shelved in the study, the steady accumulation of centuries of guilt. Nor could they explain how or why these urges surfaced beyond Lynnwood's starving origins, and those were mere suppositions. Freya found solace in their pages nonetheless. They reminded her that she wasn't alone. Not now or ever. Hundreds had felt the stirrings of that same hunger; an innate dissatisfaction with the strictures of Lynnwood, of life, where they couldn't run, or pant, or gorge themselves on grease and juice and hot, spitting fat, but were forced to walk and smile and proffer manners and civility as though it was the most natural thing in the world.

Mostly they told her about people. This, more than anything else, continued to draw her back. The same day that she fled from the Forge, she found herself again in the study. Evening light filtered through the window, catching every mote of dust, which floated on the air like grains of mud suspended in Mawley Bog. She read from many different diaries that evening, but her favourite was Ms. Andrews's, to which she always returned. Not the later entries but those that came before, showing their vicar as Freya liked to remember her. That evening, once she had read her fill of hungry poems and horrid deeds, she retrieved the leather-bound diary once belonging to their vicar and turned to a middle page.

* * *

"It was dark when I left Allerwood and started towards the village hall. Street lamps lit the pavement, the rest of Lynnwood a shapeless smudge of grey and black, but despite this I knew it was not late. I pulled back the sleeve of my coat and checked my watch anyway. It read almost six o'clock.

"Huddling deeper into the coat – an early Christmas present, from Maureen – I struggled on through the cold. The street lights guided my way, as did the sound of carol singers, faint but growing stronger. They carried on the wind. I knew the song instantly, 'Carol of the Bells'. It was a favourite from my childhood. Memories surfaced from the cold crisp of Christmases past and I remembered sitting in the front row at Midnight Mass, watching open-mouthed choristers as they celebrated the Lord with their voices.

"I walked on through the dark, coming to the village green. At first I thought to find it empty this evening. Doubtless the children had been called inside, for their dinner and bed. Then I noticed a solitary man, the homeless sort, sitting on one of the benches. I moved quickly through the darkness, feeling strangely vulnerable for the lack of company. Though never full, Allerwood Church was rarely without one person or another, come to pray, or else just stand in a House of God and be close to Him. Religious souls. 'We are a dying breed in this day and age. The Righteous Damned,' my father would have said.

"My shoes made hollow sounds against the pathway, feet moving in time to the ethereal rhythm of the choir. The church had been especially busy this afternoon, and the green seemed all the more unsettling because of this. Much to my relief it was not long before the hall grew out of the darkness ahead. I glanced back at the man on the bench as I left the green – a cursory glance, out of pity or mistrust I was not sure – but he had not moved from his seat. I thought he must be sleeping. In his own way, I supposed he was a follower of Lynnwood Green, as I was Allerwood Church. The wooden slats of the bench were his pews, the trees his pillars, the empty bottle by his feet a source of inner comfort. And though I loved the Lord, I could not help but feel something for this man and his wide, wild religion.

"My hand found the railings on the north side of the green, the gate between myself and the street swung open, but I paused. There was something more; something about this man tonight, alone on a bench, so cold, so close to Christmas. The wind picked my hair from my shoulders so that it fluttered against my face. I turned, stepped away from the railings and began walking slowly back across the green. The gate whined closed behind me.

"I have walked this way many evenings, on my way to the village meetings. In the spring it made a pleasant route, with the flowering trees, the birdsong, and lush smell of freshly cut grass. Even in the summer, when it was hotter, the walk was not unpleasant. And while the winter stripped it of leaves and life, I did not mind this much.

"I was right to suppose that the man was sleeping. His eyes were closed, his head thrown back, pale, stubbly throat exposed as though with the throes of laughter. I didn't think he had been laughing, not for a long time. Pain – exhaustion – was etched in the lines around his eyes and his shallow, sunken cheeks. I thought of a dog, which had been presented too much food, and eaten until it could not move a muscle. If his religion was the world, it was a hard one.

"Taking a few more steps, I came to a standstill beside him. I stared over him as he slept; this man, uncared for by anyone except God. I felt deeply sad. My eyes picked out more details: a bruise beneath one eye, the tattered collar of his beige coat, crumbs caught in that halfway beard. A label, sewn into his coat, read N. Roach. He was breathing deeply, I noticed; the sleep of the inebriated. I knew the sort well. Unloved, he had turned to drink to get through each day. I had not seen him in the village before this evening but I knew this to be true. What else would have brought him into my path, I, who love everyone with His unbiased eyes? It was never too late for redemption. Even the damned could be saved.

"I slipped the letter knife from around my neck. The cool chain on which it hung felt like ice against my skin. Shaped like a crucifix, I wore the object there always, a cold reminder of the Lord against my chest.

"It was the work of a moment, to press the cross gently to his forehead. I muttered a prayer. The wind rushed through the bare trees as I spoke and I heard His voice between the branches. It was grateful, justifying, and I knew I had done right by Him.

"When the figure on the bench was blessed – at peace, I thought – I replaced the chain around my neck. I wished him Merry Christmas, as across the street 'Carol of the Bells' reached its righteous climax. Then I hurried home through the night, leaving the green and the trees, the voices of the carol singers fading on the wind."

CHAPTER NINETEEN

With morning came snow and the certain knowledge that the three boys were lost to Lynnwood. Freya had known it would snow from the whiteness of the sky, but there was still no preparing for the first icy breath, bearing with it fledgling flakes. Standing in the kitchen doorway with Lizzie, she watched as Eaton and George dashed across the garden, two spirits unbridled by the breath of winter. And though there was no denying the flicker of delight that accompanied those first few flakes, she couldn't ignore the sickening realisation that the snow changed everything. The Forest, the village, the abandoned Brockenhurst line, the Old Barn, Mr. Shepherd's snowdrops and his cruel traps... Beneath the blanket of white they were all the same.

One by one, or sometimes in pairs, villagers emerged from the tree line, trudging slowly through the thickening snow. Their cheeks glowed red, their eyes sharp, narrowed perhaps from the wind, but there was a defeated look to each of them. Not because the snow had driven them inside, she thought – if anything, they looked hungrier, meaner – but because it had stripped them of an excuse to hunt beneath the boughs. Hope of finding tracks faded with the flakes. Hope of finding life faded with the cold. And so the searches were called off.

She stood with her daughter for nearly an hour while child and beast stalked each other through the garden. They talked about many things: the Knightwood Oak, which seemed to have inspired Lizzie to new heights of artistic flare, her time at school, and what the future might

119

hold for her. Lizzie told her then that she wanted to attend university. She had found the perfect course, a Fine Art degree at Winchester. Freya felt proud for her daughter, who she thought had grown into such a strong young woman. The world could teach so much but not that fierce drive; the determination to succeed, to lead the pack through the narrow spaces between the trees of Lynnwood, of life.

She realised she hadn't considered her own future for a long time. She had been enacting routines, daily rituals, but never living as Eaton lived, bounding through the snowy grass, tongue lolling, hunger burning. She liked to think she had felt those things, once, with Robert. But then he had left and with it her appetite for pleasure, indulgence, life... Until now, when she hungered as never before, when she could hardly sleep for the wild dream that filled her night-time thoughts, in which she felt so hot and happy under the trees.

A euphoria settled over her, carried on the cold flakes, until it seemed she wasn't standing in the doorway but floating there. Her daughter had moved from her side, to make them both a hot drink. Screams filled her ears; grievous animal sounds, as Mrs. Foxley stumbled past the cottage, mingled with the savage shrieks of George as he chased Eaton round and round the garden. In that moment she forgot what it meant to be human or to be beast, or whether there'd ever been a difference.

* * *

That night Freya didn't sleep well. Brandy eased the affliction, or seemed to smother it. Her mouth grew warm,

120

her limbs numb, her thoughts slowly blurred. Finally she drifted into sleep, oblivious to the silent snow, which continued to fall solemnly past her window, or the masked figure standing outside Haven House.

* * *

In her dream, winter had settled fully over the brook. Long crystals of ice hung from the branches, which were grey and bare except where algae coated them. Sunlight streamed weakly through the trees, winking faster and faster before fading completely. The last flash caught the frozen brook, then vanished, leaving the lurid blue of twilight in its wake.

She moved quickly through the trees towards the brook. Her feet crunched against the frosty floor, echoing the footsteps of her father behind her. Though the brook was frozen, she could still hear a faint trickling, of a tiny current coursing underneath. It rushed under the ice, weak and wonderful, so that the ice appeared to be moving, or melting, when everything else was still.

At the banks she seemed to stop. The air stung her chest with every needle-breath. Slowly she looked down into the dark, translucent ice. The reflection staring back surprised her; she was not a little girl, as she had first supposed, so many weeks ago. Perhaps in that first dream she had been younger. Such concerns were fleeting. She seemed to have aged with the seasons, so that a familiar face stared back: long blonde hair, pale face rouged with cold, those lupine eyes, almost angled like those of a she-wolf. For what seemed like forever she stared at her reflection, only vaguely aware of her father behind her.

A second silhouette leant over the ice. She didn't need to look to know the Bauchan had appeared at the opposite bank. She glimpsed it from the corners of her eyes; a long, pale reflection in the murky ice, and she fancied a skeleton stood across the brook from her, or something equally thin and bleached.

As before, the silhouette shifted, kneeling to dip its hands in the waters. When it encountered the ice, it paused and seemed to reconsider, hands pressing against the glassy surface. Then, fingers outspread, it began to tap, as if exploring the ice; hollow sounds in time to her beating heart.

A familiar brightness radiated from the Forest, creeping into the corners of her vision. With every tap it seemed to expand, a snowstorm filling her view, until all she could see were the human hands, and it was then, as she pondered the nature of those delicate hands, that she felt another pair on her waist, and a thought struck her as strange: if this wasn't a childhood memory, and she was not a little girl, then it couldn't be her father who grasped her from behind.

CHAPTER TWENTY

Words could hardly hope to convey Freya's primitive urges, yet somehow George managed; her little boy reducing these bold, burgeoning feelings to structured sentences. To hear him speak of them, to see them shaped by the same mouth that kissed her goodnight before bed, was the most monstrous thing...

"Lunch, darling?" she said that afternoon, moving to the refrigerator. Lizzie leafed through a magazine at the dinner table. "I'm happy to cook. Shepherd's pie? Some pork belly? I bought some spices from the market, just last week."

Without looking up from her magazine, Lizzie shrugged. "Don't worry about lunch. I'm going out."

"You're going out?"

"I'm meeting with Rachel, remember? To discuss my art project. School might be shut but the deadline's still looming."

She thought about Lizzie and Rachel. The pair often worked on their art together. Their pieces last year had been selected for an exhibition; complementary collages using media cut-outs, displaying the Forest in summer and winter. Rachel had created the summer piece, although it was Lizzie's that had struck her as the stronger; the tall, silver trees, made from newspaper headlines, stripped of their leaves, their lives, by winter's bite. They had titled the two pieces 'The Forest'. There were still some photographs from the exhibition on the school's website.

"Are you eating with Rachel?" she said.

Her daughter nodded. "I need to leave actually, or I'll be late."

"Stay in the village," Freya said, as her daughter slipped from the kitchen. "Love you." The front door closed on her words and she returned her attentions to the refrigerator.

She felt George before she heard him; the tug of his hand on her sleeve. This in itself drew her attention. She could not remember the last time he had grabbed for her.

"I feel different," he said.

Turning to her son, she pressed the back of her hand to his forehead. "Different how, darling? Is it your stomach? Your sister wasn't very well last week; I hope you haven't caught something from her..."

"No, I mean different inside," he said. "I feel bad."

She knelt to his level, taking his face in her hands. "It's all right to feel bad, George. People feel bad all the time, for lots of different reasons. It doesn't make you any less of a man, to be honest with yourself. Remember what I said before, about honesty?"

He spoke quietly into her ear. "Honesty is good?"

"Yes, honesty is good."

There was a moment's silence, in which neither of them spoke. A car roared past the kitchen window – the third that day – its engine audible long after the vehicle had vanished. The noise was jarring, out of place, belonging to the city, not their little village. Lynnwood's sounds were altogether more penetrating, the high-pitched squeal of burning swine singing again in Freya's ears. She realised George was trembling.

"It's okay, darling. It's okay, I'm here."

"I'm not scared," he said.

"Of course you're not."

"I'm not scared, really. I just feel bad, because of Andrew and the others."

"What's happened is awful, George, but it's not your fault. You must remember that. You can't blame yourself."

"But I know," he said. "I know what's happened to them, and I haven't told anyone."

He looked up at her, his wide eyes revealing many things. She saw every ache, every shining fear, every wild gleam. She saw other things too, revealed for an instant. Then he spoke, and his words were like cold hands on the back of her neck.

* * *

George remembered the afternoon well, recounting many details Freya might have thought insignificant. Was anything significant anymore except the hurried thumping of her heart, the eager wetness of her mouth, her two children?

Mrs. Welham, the woman at the head of the classroom, was a well-fed, well-to-do creature, with broad shoulders and a frame below to match. Like so many in Lynnwood she was partial to McCready's produce: bacon, pressed between slices of thick white bread each morning. In the afternoons she spread the Allwood's jam generously over warm fruit scones and when evening came her kitchen filled with the joyous glugging of Catherine's reds as it sloshed into glasses still warm from the dishwasher. Freya knew these things about the teacher not because she had seen them with her own eyes but because she hadn't; the private, impatient habits of the people of Lynnwood, revealed only through stray seeds caught between teeth, the jagged slash of red wine lips, the quivering light in their eyes.

The subject of the lesson that afternoon was Sin. George told her how animated the woman had been, her fat arms flourishing, her mouth quick. He told her about the mud that was trawled across the carpet from the wet outdoors, the smears of rain against the windowpane. As he said these things, she thought about Sin and her own lessons in the subject. She remembered Ms. Andrews's face as she preached the predatory nature of man at Sunday service, the stained-glass monsters in the windows, the churchyard of twisted statues; human figures bent low and bestial.

In the brightly-lit classroom, with the dreary rain pressing at the windows, they discussed what happened to sinners. They had been taught about Heaven and its fiery opposite lots of times before, never mind from TV and films. It didn't mean they were going to answer. To raise their hands, speak out, act know-it-all. George had long since learned the names for those people: teacher's pet, mummy's boy, tosser. Stooped in their chairs, heads held low, the class stared at Mrs. Welham. Christopher Savage dropped his biro. From the back row, somebody laughed. It was a thoughtless sound.

"You mean prison, Miss? Like that old perve in Southampton?"

"Andrew, I don't think that's appropriate –"

"My dad said he got ten years, 'cause of those photos they found –"

126

"Stop, Andrew –"

"He said they were all –"

"Stop."

The outspoken boy shrugged, loosened his tie, hunched further over his desk. Shaken, the teacher picked up her textbook. She flicked to a page and began reading aloud, scripture concerning Hell.

George knew the way they treated Mrs. Welham wasn't fair. She was much nicer than most of the other teachers. He supposed that was why they got away with it; the rest of the class, with their behaviour. The talking, the swearing, the sheer contempt. She was sensitive and they had a second sense for such things. Pack mentality, like newly-hatched spiders to their struggling prey, or the wild dogs he had watched on the Discovery Channel last week. They could sniff out the weak and the vulnerable like so much rotting flesh, smell the rank, intestinal tang of their fear. Playground scavengers.

He was reminded of a recent dream, in which he found himself in his classroom. Mrs. Morecroft stood at the front but it was his classmates who held his attention; each of them perched upright at their desks, backs straight, their faces those of famished dogs. Saliva dripped in ropes from their sly smiles, the sort that all dogs can't help but display, and pink tongues lolled from parted jaws. For the longest time it seemed that no one moved, as if waiting some unspoken direction. The air grew moist and rank with the foetid breath of the children.

Then a great horn sounded, reverberating the windows, the walls, the very particles of his blood until it boiled with anticipation and with an unspoken signal burst. He threw himself to the floor and raced from the classroom, his schoolmates hot on his heels. At first he thought he fled from them; the feral light in their eyes, their rancid breath, the yellow rot of their teeth. Then one raced past him, and another, and another, their human hands slapping the linoleum, and he chanced upon his reflection in one of the windows. He too bore the guise of a hound, his ears pricked, mouth dripping with the promise of the hunt...

Shivering, he dismissed the dream, returning his attentions to the classroom. Outside, the rain fell harder, striking the windows at a slant. There was a sub-terranean sluice as the heating behind him kicked into life. Four rows away to the front, Mrs. Welham continued talking.

"Page thirteen, everyone. Reason and Religion. Are there enough copies? Christopher, stop playing with that pen, please. Now, all together..."

A couple of children mumbled dutifully after Mrs. Welham. Most remained silent. From somewhere outside they could hear Mr. Jones, their haggard, grey-haired PE teacher, his instructive bellows echoing across the playing fields. George stared openly at the rain-flecked windows, losing himself to the bleak, watery sky. The chairs, tables and teacher of the classroom faded into a fugue of nothingness.

He thought about Hell as it was described to him. He imagined a dark place, lit with bursts of flame and shadows. Across this rocky landscape, filled with ruinous monoliths and charred, broken trees, he saw the Damned; the lost souls of the Godless; those same men and women who lied, cheated and killed in his favourite detective dramas on television. They screamed under the black sky, condemned by a higher justice; some pitiful wails, others younger, fresher, more savage sounds.

All things considered, it was strangely disaffecting. Flames weren't frightening. Neither were screams. It all seemed so made-up, so fabricated, so detached from the village he knew.

Something struck his face and he started, as if shocked. He looked around, to the right, and found himself staring into the face of Stewart Foxley. The boy's bright eyes bore into his own and George looked quickly away. His chest ached, his forehead burning from where the paper had struck, as if remembering the pain of heavier missiles; sharper, rougher, or the hot wetness of his blood.

He glanced back as Stewart mouthed something. It might have been "I love you." Or "I'll have you." He concentrated instead on Mrs. Welham.

"The Bible describes a variety of demons, monsters of metaphor used to illustrate sin. Specifically, there were seven lords of Hell. Can anyone remember them? Or find them on the page?"

He knew all about the Sins and their namesakes. He could still remember the first time his mother had explained the concept; of Heaven and Hell, right and wrong, good and bad. He knew she wasn't religious. She had made it very clear to him that their Sunday service was a different tradition. She didn't keep The Bible or The Book of Sin side by side on the mantel like Jessica Morley's parents. But she had done well to explain the concept and he thought he had understood, at least partly.

"The seven demons, anyone? Or their Sins? It's all

there, on page thirteen. The first, somebody?"

As before, nobody spoke. Mrs. Welham stared expectantly across the class and George hid his face with his sleeves. The school bell filled the silence and the classroom flew into movement; the scrape of chair legs, slamming books, animated chatter as everyone rose to leave. Chris's biro struck George on the chin, to laughter. He twitched, his face burning, and shrank inside his jumper.

"See you later, Georgie," said Chris as he sauntered behind his chair. He kicked the table, which shuddered on its legs.

"Don't forget your homework, you shit," said Andy. Then Stewart himself strode past. He smacked George on the head.

"Better run, Georgie, your mum'll be waiting at home for you."

The three of them left, surrounded by a crowd of other students, and then George was alone in the classroom. As he finished packing away his things, he realised The Bible knew nothing of Hell. Snatching his rucksack, he ran from the classroom. The school grounds swallowed him up.

* * *

Nobody remembered seeing the three boys beyond the high street, so they couldn't have known that on the day they vanished they had turned off at the disused station, or that they followed a fourth boy as he moved alone along the tracks towards the Forest. Freya only knew these things because George had told her. There were no other witnesses, except the trees themselves.

The rain had churned the grassy embankment into a mound of mud. It continued to fall, dashing grass and soil like pebbles. Winter was upon them and the nights were drawing in. It would not be long, George suspected, before his mother wouldn't let him here at all, for fear of accidents in the dark. He moved quickly, with scientific fervour, studying the gaps between the sleepers for snails and earthworms.

The three boys interrupted George just as he had sat down by the tunnel. He remembered it as though detached from his own body; staring down over the boys as they converged on him. They rushed through the rain, three dark shapes, wet and wild.

He saw himself, rising as they approached, head turned, alarmed by their whooping. His trousers were soaked through with rain and mud. He felt very cold. They were shouting things but their voices reached him distorted, as though travelling through water, or drowned beneath another sound, which was quiet at first but grew very quickly into an ancient roar, droning in his ears like a swarm of bees, except coming from the cave behind him...

He remembered pain as they pushed him back to the ground. He remembered their faces, long and pale and filled with something much older than their physical selves; a sharp disdain for rules and restraint. He remembered burning with heat, blood pounding in his ears beneath that terrible roaring, and another heat against his legs as he wet himself.

The figure emerged from the tunnel, loping across the grass like an ape. He saw pale skin, a childlike face and long arms, which snatched the three boys and broke them.

Even as its fingers curled around their flesh and that deafening roaring was cut short by snapping bones, the boys' expressions were those of ecstatic terror. Their lips twisted, their eyes shone with rainwater, wide and unknowing, and then they shone no more.

Silence sank over the clearing. George stared, unmoving, as the figure examined the bodies with its nose. Like a spider it scuttled from boy to boy, back arched, head low. Then it dragged them, one by one, backwards into the tunnel, leaving him alone beneath the empty sky.

* * *

A scream shatters the silence that has settled over the village. Nib still pressed into the paper, she pauses. Drawing a deep, tremulous breath, she stands from her note-making and moves to the window. The floor feels cold, almost icy, against her bare feet.

Two birds pick at something in the garden, beside the Griffin sculpture Robert and she had bought together in Lyndhurst. They are crows; great, black birds with marble eyes and shining beaks. Their talons bury into the thing beneath them, puncturing soft flesh, sliding past skin to the wet muscle beneath. She glances at their prey only briefly, before returning her eyes to the birds. It is recently dead, much like the rest of Lynnwood. She notes the steam, which pours from its ravaged stomach into the cold outside. Moments ago it had been one of Catherine's cats. The animals had been the first to go missing. Before Mr. Shepherd, before the boys, even before Ms. Andrews. Of course, no one had noticed at the time.

The crows make short work of the cat until it is unrecognisable. Their talons reduce it to flesh and fur and ropes of intestinal meat. Her stomach's screams join those of the frenzied birds...

She drags herself back to the dining table. Her fingers find furrows in the wood, where her pen has pressed through the paper. She follows the shallow grooves, like a blind woman reading with her fingertips. Blood brail. It is the greatest irony, that she is reduced to reading like the sightless when she sees clearly now for the first time, when words themselves mean so little anymore.

She finds the pen again. It feels strange in her hand; a relic from a different time. Somehow she resumes writing. In her mind's eye she sees only the crows; two broad, black silhouettes. She hears them even as she writes, their hungry cries ringing in her ears...

CHAPTER TWENTY-ONE

Freya knew there were no monsters, no figures in the trees, but still she felt the need to hold George tight. He trembled in her arms, his breath soft against the curve of her neck. She ran her hands down the back of his jumper, as though stroking his story away; his words wiped clean beneath the palm of her hand. At some point she closed her eyes and they stood in silence. She became aware of other things in the absence of sight; the artificial texture of his jumper against her fingertips, the boniness of his slight frame, the warmth of her own breath, over his shoulder.

Then he did a rare thing, his own arms reaching out to hug her back. They joined behind her, his hands locking, and she felt the terror of the unknown in that grasp. A child, young to the world, he was still capable of marvelling at the enormity of the sky, of fearing its emptiness, of feeling the trees and the grass and the swift-footed animals of the Forest in his blood, but was expected to ignore all these things, or deny them, for order and conscience and proper conduct. There was nothing proper, nothing natural about it. That, she thought, was the greatest contradiction of all, the truest irony in this modern world of masked, proper predators.

* * *

For Freya's sixth birthday her parents threw a small garden party. All of the children from her class were invited; her mother and she had spent a whole day making invitations, using paper and glitter and the colouring crayons from the drawer in her bedroom. And what invitations they had been! The colours, the magnificence, the fierce pride she had felt, handing them out to her friends!

She spent the afternoon making a nest from the fresh grass cuttings. The smell of the recently-mowed lawn was intoxicating, as was the sodden feel of it in her hands, the press of the summer sun against her face. Laughter filled the garden as her parents entertained the other grown-ups around the patio table.

The summer sun flashed in Freya's eyes. She began to feel hot and thirsty as she patted the mounds of grass into the nest-shape. She considered getting up to fetch some squash from the table.

A silhouette fell over her, blocking the sun from her eyes. She looked up at a girl who was making a similar grass nest across the lawn. A moment passed while they studied each other.

She remembered the shriek of the adults as their parents drank and ate and laughed into the sky, and the stillness that accompanied Catherine as she stood silently over Freya, as she reached for grass from Freya's nest, the grass that Freya had so carefully amassed for herself. She remembered standing up and pushing Catherine and kicking her; this girl, who sought to steal from her grass nest, where her imagined young would sleep and grow and writhe amid the cuttings. She had shouted and scratched Catherine with her fingers and Catherine had cried and their parents had come running to split them apart, placate them, as all children are meant to be placated. She realised this might be the earliest memory she had of Catherine. The earliest memory of her oldest friend; a memory of damp grass and drawn blood and wild faces.

* * *

Evening soon fell on Lynnwood. Lizzie returned home from Rachel's house in the fading light. Freya cooked them a mighty meal: sausages, smooth mash, mixed vegetables and dense, dark gravy. The hot, rich food would do them good, she decided. Mostly, she needed it herself; the fat, juicy sausages, sweetened with apple, the creamy potato, the crunch of the carrots – still slightly hard – between her teeth.

George and she cleared their plates. Lizzie picked at her food before scattering from the table. Freya finished the leftovers herself. There was never enough.

Alone again with her son, she forbade him from returning to the tunnel. She told him the figure was not his friend, that he was dangerous and might hurt him, if given the chance.

"But he saved me," said George.

"He didn't save you, darling. Those poor boys were in the wrong place at the wrong time."

"They hurt me," he said, "and then they couldn't hurt me anymore."

She strained inside, chest tight, unable to explain the wrongness of what had happened. Perhaps it was because she almost doubted that wrongness herself. He was her baby, after all, and they had struck him...

"They were being very cruel, George, but they needed telling off. What happened to them isn't right..."

He told her he didn't understand but that he would

stay away from the tunnel, if it was what she wanted. Then he said he was tired and that he was going to bed. She excused him from the kitchen and resumed her household ritual; clearing the table, hand washing the dishes, losing herself to those chemical suds, anything but contented.

* * *

After that day, George spoke of many dreams. He shared them openly with Freya, having learned the merits of honesty, the relief of unburdening his thoughts with another. She took solace from this realisation. Deception was another artifice. Her son, at least, seemed to have recognised this.

He dreamt first of a copse within the Forest. She knew the place well; recognisable by the Hanging Tree, of local and historical fame. Back in the forties, a village witch – Margaret Roach – had made the tree her haunt. Though she was never charged with witchcraft, it was a well-known fact about the village. Certainly, there was much conflict recorded between her goings-on and those of Ms. Andrews's parents. Allerwood parish, it seemed, did not take kindly to pagans and devil-worshippers. Many were the mornings she could be seen, walking from her cottage in the direction of the tree, a cape around her shoulders, a necklace of animal bones in one hand. She made the grotesque artefact from the remains of her dog, after it was crushed beneath the wheels of a cart, or so the guidebooks said.

Those same guidebooks recounted how Margaret hung herself in the winter of '49. Her body was left to swing from the old oak branches for three days before one resident found her and took pity. It wasn't difficult for Freya to imagine the villagers' relief at the death of the woman and her unwholesome taint on their village – the hypocrisy!

In George's dream there were three figures: the tree, a woman and a solitary magpie. In this dream the figures, which seemed to have been waiting, began to turn on one another as he approached. The magpie moved first, plucking ravenously at the Hanging Tree, drawing strips of bark, like pale flesh, from its trunk. Sap oozed from the wounds, glazing the bird's beak.

Even as the bird's beak grew more frenzied, the woman, tall and thin but glowing so brightly George couldn't see her features, fixed her shining face on the magpie. Moving towards it, like a ghost above the grass, she snatched her struggling prey in one singular motion and stuffed it into her face. There was no eating, no movement of the mouth – there was no mouth – but this didn't save the bird. It was absorbed entirely, with a muffled croak, one glistening green feather falling in its wake.

Then the Hanging Tree, wounded though it was, fixed its hungry eyes on the woman, and the sound that echoed from its broken lips rang with the enormous appetite of the Forest itself. Groaning into the dusk, which grew darker with every moment that passed, it drew the woman into its mouth; that gaping chasm of empty blackness, from which no things escaped...

Another time George dreamt of night and a snowstorm falling over the village. At first he ran outside into the path of the snow, relishing the delicate kiss of each flake against his skin. It built up on the ground and crunched beneath his feet, a cold carpet of pure white. He opened his mouth, tasting the flakes on his tongue.

Other figures began emerging from their homes; thin silhouettes, illuminated in the doorways of their cottages. They too moved amid the snow, faceless and laughing, swaying like dead branches in the wind.

The snow continued to fall, thicker and faster, until it seemed to move against his face and, looking up, he realised the flakes were tiny insects; flies, made entirely from frost. They fell frantically from the night, moving in vast, swirling clouds, swarms of droning ice. They crawled across flesh, their feet scratching skin, and where they landed the villagers grew gaunt until the white street was filled with white bodies; the last dance of the snow dead, grinning under the yellow light of the moon.

He dreamt of the dog-children again, and the wild hunt through the corridors, and often of that afternoon by the tunnel, when the three boys had been taken. Freya tried to console her son, running her hand through his hair and holding him in her arms, but he hadn't finished talking. As though she had unstopped something inside of him, he continued to speak, his lips spilling ever darker dreams.

And each time, he said, no matter the nature of the dream, he would find himself back in his bedroom, in the dark and the cold, with the imagined movement of a figure at his window; a streak of white, glimpsed then gone from where it had pressed up against the glass. His friend from the tunnel, watching over him.

CHAPTER TWENTY-TWO

It was still light when Freya left for Catherine's house. The sun shone salmon pink above the tree line. She moved quickly through the twilight towards the cottage, her boots against the snow the only sound down the street. This time no curtains twitched. The houses stared back at her, somehow older, less cared-for. She wasn't sure that she preferred the stillness.

Relief filled her at the sight of the cottage. She hurried the rest of the way down the street and up the pathway. Catherine would know what to say. They would open a bottle and collapse in her sofas and talk and laugh as they had done for nearly forty years. She could almost smell the robust wine, oaky and delicious in her mouth.

As she stepped up to the door, she realised that she really could smell wine. She noticed the curtains were shut. She also noticed several bottles, nestled in the bushes. She might not have seen them except for the smell and the way they caught the fading light. Anxiety fluttered inside her.

"Catherine?" she called. She knocked against the door, then waited a minute. "Catherine, are you in?"

She entered the cottage using the key Catherine had given her when she had gone abroad last summer and asked Freya to keep an eye on the cats. The key slid smoothly into the lock, turning quickly in her hand.

Movement sounded behind the door as someone sprang back. Only moments behind, Freya heard footfalls against the old wood, glimpsed a pale shape as it disappeared into the kitchen.

"Catherine?" she said, "Catherine, what's the matter?"

When Catherine spoke, her voice was like a hiss. "Go away!"

She followed the voice and the vanishing shape into the kitchen. Her throat was tight, her stomach sick. She felt as though everything she had eaten these past months was swimming inside her, pushing at her skin, threatening to rise up into her mouth. Had the hunger reached her friend? Had it claimed Catherine?

The cottage was in disarray. More bottles, mostly empty, cluttered the work-surface. She noted sheets of paper, scrunched into tight balls beside the bin. A slab of brie festered on a chopping board. Beside it, a cheese-knife glistened blue and green.

"Catherine, where are you?"

"Please, go away," said the voice again. She followed it to the wine cellar. The door was locked. She touched it, lay her head against it.

"You know you shouldn't drink alone, Ms. Lacey."

After a moment, Catherine replied. "You know you shouldn't drink at all, Ms. Rankin."

"Are you going to tell me what the matter is?" she said.

Laughter echoed from the cellar. It didn't sound like Catherine. "The matter? You might as well ask me the point of cats again."

"We never did decide on that," Freya said.

More laughter bubbled up from behind the door. "We decided you were a bitch, remember?"

"Ms. Lacey! That's hardly something to call someone from behind closed doors."

"You're a bitch, I'm a bitch, the whole world is full of

bitches." Catherine's voice was sharp, acidic. It matched the stench of the kitchen. "Isn't that the point? The point of it all?"

"The point of what?"

"Life!" hissed Catherine. Something smashed in the wine cellar. "To breed, to feel a man between your legs, to drop screaming children, one after the other, to mother them like they're you, like they're a part of you, crawling hungry and bloody across the floor?"

Laughter degenerated into sobs, then bubbled back again until Freya could hardly distinguish between the two. She felt herself beginning to cry. "Don't do this to yourself," she said quietly. "Catherine, don't."

"How can't I, when it's all around me? All I see anymore is the hunger in people's eyes, the desire burning there, a hunger for life that I can never know. I can never know it!"

Freya choked back her voice. "There's other things too, Catherine. Think about it. Think about me."

"Think about you?"

"Think about love."

Freya felt hot and dizzy from the tears and the heady aroma of wine. Reds and whites and half-drunk pinks had mixed into a kaleidoscope of rank smells, which caught in the back of her throat. Her eyes fell back to the brie, rotting slowly on the side. She found she couldn't look at it.

"Love is nothing," muttered Catherine. "Love means nothing."

"Don't you love me?"

"I... can't," she said. "I can't have children and I can't

love you! The rest of the village has let go and I can't! So tell me, what's the point?"

Freya sank slowly to her haunches against the door. She pressed her thumb to the wood, remembering a promise, pricked in blood. She thought she might lose herself wholly to tears, but instead swallowed them down. Eventually she managed words.

"Did you ever find Merlot?" she said.

"No."

"She's the point, Catherine. Merlot's the point. Follow in her footsteps. Go, be with her." Freya felt herself smiling. "You always were more of a cat woman."

CHAPTER TWENTY-THREE

In the hallway of Haven House the next morning, Freya slipped into her wellies. Her Parka felt dry against her skin and strange, as though she shouldn't be wearing it. It was a moment before she slid it over her arms and zipped it up to her chest.

She had to know the truth of George's story, to verify what had happened to those boys in the tunnel, if not for peace of mind then to sate her own curiosity. There could be no peace of mind, not while she still belonged to the village. There was only her hunger, which she knew would never end. Eaton paced around her legs, his tail wagging, anticipation shining in his eyes. She thought he looked sad. As she attached the leash to his collar, she wondered about the emotional capacity of the dog. Was he really sad? Or was she just imagining the upset in his eyes? He had food, water, shelter and love...

She opened the door and stepped out into the bracing cold. They moved quickly through the village, woman and dog. Snow fell softly around them. She thought of George, of the snow he had dreamt, then insects and hungry swarms, swirling in the air. They passed few people on the way. She exchanged a furtive glance with a teacher from the school. The man was white with cold, his eyes dark, narrow. His vanishing footsteps crunched in the snow behind her. Once or twice a curtain twitched, but when she turned to look it was too late. Once she thought she saw a pale face, staring at her through a window, but only once. All other times there was nobody there, and after that she let the curtains twitch and didn't look again. She passed through the village, across the high street and the abandoned station, and walked towards the trees.

As the last time, she followed the overgrown tracks. They proved slippery with ice, so she walked across the embankment, where the cold and snow had made the mud hard. She released Eaton from his lead. He bolted across the grass after some invisible prey or, she thought, the silhouette of her son, who she pictured running ahead, peering between the metal slats, moving ever closer to the yawning mouth of the tunnel.

She followed the apparition through the snow. Often he stopped to examine the unseen, and she realised she was smiling; her little boy, lost and fascinated in equal measure at the monstrous size of the world around him and the unknown things within. They were all lost, really. No one person truly knew their place in Lynnwood, domesticated by school and society into good, orderly citizens.

It was madness, she realised, faltering in her step. It was insanity, branded the norm. Her eyes studied her son a second longer, then he dissipated under a flurry of snowflakes and she watched Eaton instead as he raced across the heathland. The sadness was gone from his eyes. His paws churned clumps of snow.

The tunnel mouth seemed wider than she remembered. It whistled with wintry breath and an undercurrent of something else. She smelled the foetid stench, so much like spoiled meat, and her face fell. Inside she seethed; the maternal against the hungry, the social against the wild, the wrong against the right.

Another gust of wind brought the stench renewed, and she winced. Eaton must have caught the smell too, for he inched past her, his ears flat, one paw in front of the other. What did it mean, if the three boys rotted in there? They had lives once, futures, mothers of their own. She could still hear Mrs. Foxley's wails from when she had passed Haven House after the searches were called off. They were honest sounds, heartfelt and human as anything Freya had come to expect.

And yet everything had changed now. She saw Lynnwood for what it was, and in the village there were only two sorts: those that hunted and those who were their prey. One fed, the other was fed upon. And in doing so they nurtured the hunters, who grew strong and full beneath the Forest canopy, or the oaken beams of their cottages, bright and indomitable as the constellation Orion itself...

Inside the tunnel nothing moved that she could see. The darkness was dense and velveteen. Frost clung to the tunnel mouth like ravenous spittle and, around the base, more snowdrops broke through the blanket of white. Nature's bouquets, commemorating the three boys who festered within and the role they played in the insatiable cycle of life.

Cold and contemplative, she didn't notice the trap, concealed in the snow. A single, heavy crash echoed across the clearing, followed by Eaton's whimpers. Arms stiff, chest frozen with fear, she rushed towards the wounded dog even as something else darted from the darkness of the tunnel. Much closer than Freya, it reached Eaton first, and seeing the skeletal figure in the overcast light she faltered, slipping in the snow.

It had been Mr. Shepherd, once. She had seen it before, watching her from his workshop. But under the wintry light it looked horrible. Its naked flesh seemed blue and pink. Ribs pressed from its chest, its eyes wild behind that monstrous mask, which was at once ornate and revolting.

She struggled to her feet and started towards Eaton. His head lolled wildly, eyes mad, as the snow became red around him. It was darkest around his forelegs, where the metal had mangled his flesh, becoming paler and icier as it diffused into the flakes.

Long fingers reached for the dog's head. He snapped once, instinctively, yellow teeth flashing from black gums, then the figure grasped his head and twisted. A crack, like thawing ice, echoed in her ears.

Silence settled over the clearing as Freya fell upon the man. She remembered the press of it beneath her, the surprising softness of its skin for one so thin and hard. Her face felt hot, burning with anger and sadness and a thrill she had never known. This was a new instinct and an old one, no less bred into her blood. The figure might have kicked her, or thrown her back, she couldn't be sure. It was strong. It thrashed wildly beneath her, and then she was on her back in the snow, the breath knocked from inside her. Tears ran into her hair.

The roar of the Forest filled her ears. Turning sideways, she watched as the figure dragged Eaton's body into the tunnel. Then a howl emerged from the darkness, half human, half beast, and as she crawled to her feet and staggered toward the village it was answered by another from the trees, and another, and another, until the

147

morning air filled with cries of wild hunger.

* * *

Lynnwood blurred around her as she ran. She might have been moving through banks of fog, or a distant memory. In many ways, the village was a memory now. Lynnwood as she had known it all her life no longer existed. The streets, the trees and the stone-cold tiles of their kitchen floors were all bathed in invisible blood; monstrous deeds committed by monstrous people, dried and flaky in the cracks between the stone, or soaked into the soil beneath their feet. She felt lost, stripped of the society she had been raised to depend on. It had been torn from around her; a lamb, devoured by Aesop's wolves, leaving her naked and vulnerable in the cold and the snow...

CHAPTER TWENTY-FOUR

It might have been midday when Freya found herself outside Catherine's house. The cottage was still. She stared numbly at the building, which meant so much and so little, Eaton's lead hanging limply by her side. She knew Catherine had gone, to be as the others in the Forest. She could tell just from looking at the house. Still she walked slowly up the path to the oak wood door and knocked.

She didn't know quite how old the house was, or how long the Laceys had lived there, only that it had stood for hundreds of years at least. Families had lived out their lives behind the grey stone of its walls; their loves, their hates, their tender moments and cruel words imprinted on that stone for as long as people living remembered. She knew Catherine's pain when, late for school one morning, she had stubbed her toe on a table-leg. She heard the echoes of Catherine's laughter when they had discovered a dirty book in her father's study. How they shrieked at the thought of learned Mr. Lacey, nose-deep in those pages! She remembered the quiet sound of the floorboards beneath their feet as Catherine had leaned in to kiss her, the thrill that had coursed through her as their lips brushed together that first time. It had been their last day of school and her breath was hot with celebratory wine. The taste, she knew, had remained with Catherine for decades afterwards.

She knew the sounds of grief, when Catherine's parents passed away, of joy, when she had bought Merlot, and the animal screams of birth when the cat had produced her litter. She knew tears and smiles and the warmth of desire and the walls knew all these things too. A lifetime witnessed and remembered.

She used her key to enter the cottage. The inside was just as she remembered it. The hallway had been tidied recently. Six empty wine bottles stood beside the door. She smelled lavender and loneliness and realised she was breathing heavily.

She moved into the front room. The scarlet curtains were stark against the whiteness of outside. Some books had been left open on the coffee table, their spaces vacant in the bookcase. They looked like poetry collections. She didn't read them but turned to inspect the rest of the house, revisiting the rooms and retracing the steps she had walked a hundred times.

The bedrooms were perfectly made. The bathroom too appeared to have been thoroughly cleaned. On descending into the wine cellar she found it empty. Where before there had been stacks of wine, cases of bottles older than she, now there was only darkness and the skeletal framework of the racks. The air was sweet and vinegary on her tongue.

The kitchen was cold. The whole house was cold, as though Catherine alone had warmed it with her lips, her eyes, her wild, drunken laughter. On the work-surface, beside the knife block, she found a piece of paper. It was a page, torn carefully from a book. A lipstick had been used to weigh it down.

For several minutes she read silently from the page. Then she turned and walked out of the cottage, closing the door behind her. On the doorstep she smelled the lingering aroma of lavender. She fancied she heard laughter and crying and the mewling of a cat. Then she left.

Marry me, my Lady,
By the Forest's edge,
Hear the trickling of the stream
As we, as one, are wed.

Marry me, my Lady,
By the Forest's side,
Hear the roaring of the trees
As we, as one, are wed.

Marry me, my Lady,
By the Forest's kiss,
Hear the silence of the leaves
As we, as one, are wed.

* * *

She has almost caught up with herself. It could not have been a week, days perhaps, since Eaton stepped in the jaws of the trap. He flashes behind her eyes, his auburn fur matted with blood, as though the colour seeped out of him with the passing of his life into the snow. She misses him more than she can express in words, or through the nib of a pen. A memory resurfaces, which she had thought lost. She is watching a puppy as it crosses their sitting room, head low, ears flat with the curiosity of youth. He is awkward-looking, like the foals born to the Forest in spring. He grew into his limbs, his speed, her love; a constant reminder of that last meal with Robert, when she had first decided they would one day get a dog. And now he has gone. They have both gone. There is almost nothing left, to remind her who she was.

She clutches her chest, feeling the texture of her clothes – these had mattered, once – then the hardness of her chest beneath. She traces her ribs with her fingers, reminding herself that when all else fails she is flesh and blood and sweat and bone and hot, wet breath...

Eaton was all these things, and now he is none of them, even his bones snapped and sucked clean by the man that had been Mr. Shepherd. Her stomach growls, and she hears Eaton in her mind, lips drawn back, teeth bared, and then it is not Eaton but Mr. Shepherd, jaw set, mouth red, and then her son, his eyes sharp in his pale face, mouth open, a hungry shout tearing from his throat.

She does not know for certain if Mr. Shepherd was always in the tunnel. She does not know whether he visited her son at night, whether it was he who bequeathed him the brooch from Ms. Andrews's grave. She does not know whether it was he who protected her son from those boys, who dragged their bodies into the tunnel and ate from them, or whether it was George himself, her little George, who fed on their flesh, every bite a rebuke against their bullying, against school, against uniform and smart shoes and Sunday service and a world that neither loved or understood him, but expected him to comply all the same.

Her chest rises and falls quickly beneath her arms. Her ribs are hard, her body shaking. This is not the first time she has considered his role in Lynnwood's darkness, but it is the first time she has faced it. Inside, she has always known, always suspected. They all grow lean and hungry. Why should her son be any different? Nothing else could have driven her back to the tunnel that day, where the trees grew so close, except to stare with her own eyes into the abyss where her son had simultaneously found and lost himself.

Another figure flashes behind her eyes and she starts as, outside, pink sky turns to midnight blue. It is her daughter's face, so similar to her own. It stirs more feelings inside of her. Pride struggles to surface above the forest of primitive drives, which are so strong now. Pride and sadness enough to dredge her from instinctual descent, for just one moment. One moment is all she needs, before she is free to run as the dogs through the trees. One moment of remembrance for one solitary girl, who, when the rest of Lynnwood succumbed to their wilder instincts, fought a silent battle with her hunger, unnoticed by all.

CHAPTER TWENTY-FIVE

The howling of the figures in the trees showed no signs of stopping. Freya fell against the inside of her front door, silencing the wind and the screams. In the hallway, all was still. Lamplight shone from the kitchen and a soft ticking reached her ears, of the grandfather clock to her right. She realised she still held Eaton's leash in one hand. Her fingers were white, where they clasped it tightly. Slowly she placed it where it belonged, on the coat-pegs with her Parka.

"George," she called. The word was followed by movement upstairs, as he stepped onto the landing. The stairs creaked three times beneath as he began to descend.

"Hello?" he said. His face appeared over the banister.

She realised she didn't know why she had called him. There was nothing she could say to explain what had happened. "Nothing, darling. Just... Nothing."

He stared at her a second longer, then started to withdraw from the stairs.

"George, wait."

"Yes?" he said, reappearing.

"Have you seen your sister?"

"She's in her room," he said.

"Thank you."

She didn't ask him what he was doing upstairs in his room. Nor did she mention Eaton. Alone she moved through the cottage, inspecting every room, as though viewing them for the first or last time. In the sitting room, her eyes lingered over the case of butterflies. She stared at their delicately preserved wings, their withered bodies and fading colours. They were beauty and revulsion, change and growth and colour, captured in the glittering scales of their wings, and she had hung them from her wall, as though to remind herself of these things, to celebrate them. In the kitchen the black mass of the AGA held her attention, a testimony to man's appetite for containment. He bound his hunger to the flames of the cooker in an attempt to manage it, just as he displayed decaying remnants of the wild in cases on his walls.

In the bathroom, she studied herself in the antique mirror, as her mother had done so often before her. She wondered if they saw the same things now, if that was why Harriet had spent so long diligently masking herself beneath make-up and blusher each morning.

The cottage sounded with movement as she exited the bathroom and crossed the landing. She might have been walking through a dream; the haze of outside having followed into her home. George had fallen asleep on his bedroom floor, beside the window. She left him where he lay, curled up like an animal in its den.

She knocked at Lizzie's door. When there was no answer she knocked again. Still there was no response, so she pushed the door open and stepped inside.

The room was dark with night. Strange silhouettes leapt out at her; sculptures, illuminated in moonlight. She looked past the twisted fey figures, the screaming face casts, the abstract shapes that she realised with growing concern might have been mouths; papier mâché versions of the lost brooch –

Her daughter lay on the floor. Where George was curled comfortably into his chest; however, she was sprawled against the wood. Freya saw for the first time how pale Lizzie looked beneath the light of the moon, how thin her arms had become; like sticks of bone, her face gaunt, as though stripped of flesh and life.

She rushed to her daughter and gathered her in her arms. She was cold and hard to touch, and proved horribly light when she lifted her to the bed. A thin line of blood emerged from her nose, where she must have knocked herself. It was brown in the dark and crusty when she tried to wipe it away. How long her daughter had been lying there she couldn't tell. All she knew was the terrible state of the girl, who, it seemed, had denied her simple hunger at every turn, where everyone else had indulged it.

* * *

When Lizzie woke some hours later, she shared her private hell with Freya. It was a story of denial, driven to extremes by the growing hunger inside. There was no escaping the cycle of eating and purging. It was, in itself, all devouring; sapping Lizzie's strength, her health, her life. Only her will remained, and what an iron will it was, to maintain such strictures, to uphold her monstrous habits even as they ate her up, pound by pound! If she wouldn't feed the hunger then it would feed on her, until there was nothing left. Mother and daughter wept together, and hugged, and Lizzie unburdened herself further.

At first, she said, she hid the changes easily. They were slow and she was resourceful. She wore loose clothing and blamed tiredness on late nights, or too much pressure at school. Still, her friends looked slimmer than her. The boys at school followed Rachel as dogs to a scent. It seemed demeaning and yet she craved those base attentions, their lingering eyes on her body, their noses sniffing her scents. If only they would look! She couldn't remember a time before A-levels, before reflections in the mirror, before complex carbohydrates and glossy magazines. Reduced to these things, she was not a person. She might as well not have existed.

Food, she said, began to lose its appeal. She noted the way spots of grease swam on the surface of gravy. Meat revolted her. This was no moral choice, no personal preference, as Freya's vegetarianism had once been – how long ago that seemed now. Lizzie spoke of plucked chicken like drowned men's flesh; bare and white and bloated. Sausages glistened with fat. Bacon shrivelled and grew hard. Even as Freya celebrated her new-found hunger with cooked breakfasts each morning these sickened her daughter, so that she barely touched them, and in private regurgitated what little had passed her lips.

"How could you do this to yourself?" Freya said, when her daughter had finished speaking. "Boys don't want *this*. Nobody wants this!"

"It wasn't about the boys," she said, shrinking into her covers. "That was just how it started. But then it became more. I started getting hungrier. It felt like I was losing control and the worse that got, the more I wanted to fight it. And when I couldn't, when I couldn't cut out food altogether, I had to throw it up to get it out of me."

They continued to argue, her daughter's expression so much like the hares', caught in the headlights on the road through the village.

"I don't understand," said Freya. "This isn't normal, darling. Your body needs food to grow, to live. You know this!"

"It's under control!" she said.

"It isn't, Lizzie! Let me get you something to eat."

"No."

"Please," she said, "Lizzie. You're starving yourself."

"I can't lose control! Look at the rest of the village! Look at what they're turning into, at what they've become!"

"It's normal," said Freya, and even as she spoke she realised that she was right. Lynnwood had always taken pride in its rich array of produce. Temptation had always been near. Breads, cheeses, wines and preserves; the village expressed itself through the unique brand of its New Forest flavours, as all places do, unconsciously or otherwise. There were the Allwood's jams, Catherine's wines, McCready's meats, never mind Lynnwood's wilder appetites, which said more about the village than words ever could. The revelation seemed to rise through her, dizzy and distancing. "It's normal to feel hungry. It's normal to want boys, to feel confused and scared, but that's what I'm here for. To talk to you, to help you, to be your mother. The only thing that isn't normal is this." She reached out to touch her daughter's arm. For a second she graced the skin, cold and hard again, before it vanished into the bedcovers.

"It's normal," Freya said, and the last vestiges of doubt faded from her own mind. "You must be starving."

Her daughter's sallow eyes rose to meet hers, and in the darkness of her bedroom, swaddled in her sheets, she nodded.

Freya stayed with Lizzie all night while she slept. At some
point she also fell asleep, her daughter wrapped in her
arms. It felt good to hold her close, impossibly good, as
though holding her somehow made up for the weeks of
disregard. She felt stronger, more whole, completed by
the closeness of her offspring.

They woke before dawn to shouting. At first she was
confused, still deep in her dream by the brook. Then she
realised the shouting was real. Lizzie was recoiled into the
bedsheets and the sound coming from outside. Moving to
the window, she stared down at the street and the man
crouched in the middle of the road. Stripped of clothes
and humanity he could have been anyone. It was the
mask that betrayed him. He continued to shout; wordless
noises, wild and unchallenged.

Then a second voice reached her ears, not from the
street or the village but the room next door. It was a small
voice, high and raw, like a feral cat screaming into the
light blue of dawn. Each scream resonated inside her.
Time seemed to slow, everything else fading into the
background. All that mattered were those screams, which
she realised then came from George's bedroom. She
rushed from the window and Lizzie's room, across the
landing and into her son's room. George was nowhere in
sight. She raced to the open window, tearing back the
curtains in time to see him vanishing with Mr. Shepherd
into the village.

She stood at the window, watching him as he raced

from view. She wasn't especially upset, as she thought she should have been. Nor was she happy. Instead she felt a surge of relief that she couldn't hope to explain. Her son, at least, was free now.

CHAPTER TWENTY-SIX

"A thin, delicate figure, with wings like glass and wide black eyes, Gluttony is the youngest of the Seven Sins. Her Court and she drift languidly through the forests of the world, accompanied by mellifluous music and the intoxicating scent of spring. Yet they are not to be underestimated, for when night falls, a feverish hunger descends on the Sin and they erupt, irresistible as the tide, through the undergrowth with their bows and spears and bloody, nail-bitten claws. They slash and maul, searching out the beasts of the forest to devour, with bare hands gorging themselves, sating their yearning hunger with raw flesh and slurping down still-warm blood."

Description of 'The Forest' by Elizabeth Rankin, on display at Hollybush Manor.

* * *

Freya woke again beside her daughter. For one moment of uncertainty, she wondered whether she had dreamt her son's escape. Then she saw the shining white of winter outside, felt her daughter trembling beside her, the clammy heat that prickled her skin, and she knew it had been real.

They left the house together. Lizzie followed obediently and Freya wondered whether the girl was as drained as she. They moved quickly through the morning snow, Lizzie's shoes making compact sounds with each tread. Freya had forgone footwear. Her feet were cold, then painful, then numb enough that she couldn't feel them. She moved soundlessly beside her daughter.

Smoke continued to pour from behind McCready's

barn, as it had done now for over a week. The smoke tickled her nose almost as soon as they reached the high street, and she picked up her pace through the village. It smelled of ash and burned flesh, luring her towards the farmhouse, as though she needed encouragement.

When they reached McCready's cottage, they found the door open. She didn't enter to inspect the inside but headed around the back towards the Old Barn.

The structure towered over the farmhouse and she knew from old photographs that it had stood for many years, long before John McCready had come to Lynnwood. To the best of her knowledge he housed his pigs in there, along with various pieces of equipment. Today it was silent.

They spoke of nothing as they approached the place behind the barn. The place where the village children had used to play safely, away from the village but not so far that they intruded on the trees. Her vision blurred as she lost herself to smells and sounds and the growing pressure inside. She took her daughter's hand as they walked.

Rounding the barn, they encountered a field of charred pigs. They stopped where they stood and regarded the sight. Freya's stomach clenched even as her daughter's grasp on her hand did the same. The shapes that dotted the field were black and twisted, their bones buckled from heat, and all of them were grinning where they lay in the withered grass. At the other end of the field they spied McCready. They watched as, bent low, he set light to another of the animals. She could just make out his spidery figure, the can of lighter fluid and the fierce fire that followed. A gust of wind brought the acrid smell and with it the sound of spitting fat. He seemed to be screaming: "Mary! Mary!"

They converged on the old man and his pigs. Those nearest had not yet been burned, their porcine skin pale with cold, with death. Even before they reached him, Freya's mouth began to moisten, her eyes narrow with eagerness. Her daughter shared a similar sharp expression.

This close, the fires were intense. They crackled with ravenous glee enough to match that inside her. Still McCready screamed. The heat pressed against her face, blasting her skin, as mother and daughter fell upon the nearest animal. At first they were tentative, pressing their hands to the pig's swollen belly. Though it hadn't been burned, its skin was warm and dry from the nearby fires. Much of the hair had been singed from its back and sides, so that only a few crisp strands remained. She began to press harder, her fingers sinking into the flesh as though massaging it.

Seemingly satisfied, they gorged themselves on the pig. The field around them faded into nothingness. Freya knew only heat from the fires, the rubbery feel of the flesh in her mouth, tough and slippery between her teeth. Sometimes her daughter's hand met hers, sometimes another pair, as McCready crouched to join them. Her eyes watered, where smoke blew into their faces, but she didn't care. There was no stopping this revelry. She felt free at last; of Lynnwood, of Robert, of artifice and of conscious thought. All she knew was the wild abandon of feasting and the deep gratification that every mouthful brought.

* * *

One by one they broke off from the pig, momentarily sated, and sank into the snow. Much of it had melted from the constant heat, leaving sodden slush across this part of the field. Slowly she returned to herself, her sides aching, mouth stained with worse than blood. Though she remembered herself in these moments, she also knew that she had changed; that she wasn't the same woman she had been before, or her daughter, or the man beside them. They were something less now, or more. She was filled, completed by the flesh of the animal in their midst.

Only once the fires died, and the cold became too much, did she rise to her feet with her daughter. McCready remained on the ground, thin but bloated. He seemed to have stopped screaming, reduced to rasping breaths. The wind took her hair and cooled the stains against her face. She moved sluggishly back through the village with her daughter, to the place that had been their home.

CHAPTER TWENTY-SEVEN

Freya couldn't say what drove her back to the Vicarage in those last days. It felt important to see the place one more time, so that she could leave it fully behind her. As with her own cottage the day before, she moved through the lifeless building, seeing and remembering. Ghosts assumed themselves in the shadows; two women enjoying scones and brandy and civil conversation. Whispered words carried on the dusty air. She found that she felt strangely at home in the darkness, in a building where she had always previously felt stifled.

The last diary she read was her own, "Freya Harriet Heart" written in small letters across the cover. She hadn't been surprised when she found it in the bookcase. She thought that she remembered it, from years gone; the escape of a schoolgirl with a sick father and a mother who both loved and hated herself.

The diary was small, and irregularly kept, as anything required of a child was. She flicked through it, reluctant to read too deeply. She didn't recognise this girl anymore. This was someone else's life, someone else's memories. Still, she couldn't leave without looking inside. She owed herself that much.

There were the accounts of horror that each Midwinter brought. She had expected these, given what she already knew. She read of the figure at their sitting room window, the year Harriet had first taught her to bake. The year after, she noted four children missing from her class. Her parents said their families had left the village but she had found bones and scraps of school uniform, when playing with the dogs on one of their walks through the Forest. She read of the night her bed-ridden father had vanished, and how he had fled from the cottage, Harriet close behind him, howling as he staggered for the trees.

It was not these accounts that struck her but the human details she found most affecting, as though seeing them from the other side and remembering their tenderness.

She recalled the day Catherine and she had followed Marcus Gillingham home from school. His parents had owned one of the bigger houses near to the church, and it was quite a walk from the Manor.

Catherine and she had lusted for him in the way young girls are both intrigued and repulsed by boys. He must have known they were following him but he never turned around. That seemed only to have incited their intrigue further. Why wouldn't he look at them? Why couldn't he see them? She heard her own voice, so much like her daughter's the night before, saw her eyes filled with that same frenetic fear. It didn't matter that the other boys were interested, or that not a week later Robert Rankin, from Mrs. Lovejoy's class, would ask to walk her home, offering his jacket when it started to rain.

She read and remembered the time she had mixed up the salt with the sugar when baking cakes with her mother for the village market. They hadn't realised their mistake until Joan – Ms. Andrews to her, then – had taken a generous bite out of a cherry scone. Freya's laughter, she was told, had been heard as far as the Old Barn.

She had written of the day their Cocker Spaniels, Ralph and Jack, had attacked another dog. After that they had been put down. They were "unsafe," her father had insisted, "what if that had been your dog, Freya? What if they'd gone for you?" She hadn't thought that fair. They were only doing what came naturally. It had made no difference in the end. She was allowed to say goodbye, to stroke them both one last time, their tails wagging, blissfully oblivious to the fate that awaited them at the veterinary centre in Lyndhurst. She thought she had grown up a little that day. She had written as much in the diary.

She glanced over a dozen such intimate moments, until she felt sick from sentimentality and could read no more. Then she placed the diary back where she had found it on the shelf, and she left the Vicarage and didn't return again.

* * *

With night came hunger and the dream that had afflicted her for so long. It began as always; with her running through the trees. Her feet dashed icy puddles. The light glittered in the branches overhead, then flashed and was gone. Shadows rushed from the spaces between the trees, stretching across the floor, reaching for her and the elf rings she knew were there but couldn't see for the snow. Footsteps crunched behind her, as the second figure gained ground.

The brook appeared ahead, frozen but lively with the current underneath. She moved across the bank, to where ice met soil, and knelt, as always, to drink. When her hands encountered the sheet of ice they paused, fingers pressing curiously. She knew without looking that the Bauchan across the brook was doing similarly. She had

167

seen it a dozen nights already; its cold, red fingers testing the dark ice.

She looked anyway. She was helpless not to in this place, this dream, which was nothing compared to the real brook and yet felt so real all the same. Her eyes rose slowly to the figure opposite, expecting whiteness to expand her vision, breaking from the brook or the snow, as it had always done before she could see properly. Only this time, no whiteness came. She looked up, seeing those hands still pressed to the ice, following slender arms, a familiar blouse and then the face, her face, staring back at her across the Forest. She looked drawn, bloodless, as though the cold had numbed her entire body. It was all she could do to stare at herself, crouched like an animal beside the brook, fingers scratching at the ice. She was the figure. She was the Bauchan!

The sound of running feet slowed to a walk. Then the figure, who she had once mistakenly thought her father, strode up behind her and slipped his hands around her waist. She felt those hands, so warm against her stomach, even as she watched them on the opposite bank and she saw that they weren't her father's but Robert's, and it was he who stood behind her.

Fear and uncertainty took hold of her. She couldn't remember this, even as it played out before her. She remembered the blouse though, which she had worn on their last night together, and her bare feet, and the way in which she crouched beside the brook like a thirsty dog. Then she heard him talking in her ear.

"Freya," he said, "Freya. It's me, Robert. It's your Robert."

168

She squirmed, tried to spin round, wriggling in his grasp, but his arms became something more, a fierce grip on her stomach.

"Freya, it's okay. It's going to be okay. I'm going to look after you. You can fight this. You can fight this!"

She kicked harder now, pushing off from the bank with her feet. They scrunched up against the snow and the hard soil beneath, then lashed out. Through unknowing eyes, she watched as the couple across the brook tumbled to the floor. She snarled, spat, at the mercy of the Midwinter Frenzy all those years ago. It had claimed her once already! Her mind raced with fear. She must have fled the house after the meal. Her hunger must have drawn her to the trees. He must have followed her.

He wouldn't give up on her. His arms said that much, as they continued to grip her tightly. She could hardly breathe in the stranglehold, the figure opposite writhing horribly, and yet she knew he was trying to help. He was trying to contain her, to save her from herself and the others who stalked the trees on this night alone.

Her head flew back and knocked into his face. His grip loosened. She thrust forward, her toes finding purchase on the ground, and struggled to her feet. One foot stepped onto the ice, which cracked beneath her weight.

The man on the ground scrabbled towards her.

"Freya, listen to me. Listen to my voice. This isn't you!"

She heard him and the words that spilled from his mouth, but they meant little to her like this. She had only eyes for the black wetness beneath his nose, the stink of his sweat, the ragged breaths that came from his throat. Looking into her eyes he seemed to sense this. He

169

staggered to his feet, his hands raised in front of him.

"Freya," he said. "Stay with me. I want to help. I'm here to help you. I love you. You know I love you."

She rushed at him through the night, one part remembering, the other reliving. He turned and ran. Every second stretched out as she chased him through the trees. She felt the snow between her toes, the flakes that had begun to fall against her face. Her chest ached with longing; to have him in her hands and her mouth, to feel his skin against hers, his heat, his taste on her tongue. The Forest was a blur of black and white.

She caught him near Mawley Bog, beneath an alder tree. Moonlight reflected off the frozen water, bringing his face to stark relief. She glanced at it only once and then it was forgotten, in favour of hands and teeth and the inescapability of her hunger.

CHAPTER TWENTY-EIGHT

Just as that first taste of meat had driven her to Allerwood Church, so Freya found herself once more among the headstones. Statues rose around her; some weeping angels, others Sin in its various guises. She moved between the angels and the demons, knowing full-well that neither were honest depictions. There were no divine forces, no hellish creatures, only beasts of the earth, with their feelings and their drives, however base or noble. It didn't matter. None of it mattered. The church was another lie, founded to keep the residents of Lynnwood happy in their lives, to keep them placid, when underneath they seethed with instinct.

She left the statues behind and moved across the churchyard. There, on the very outskirts, just off the gravel path, one headstone stood, no higher than a boy. A bouquet rested at its base, withered with frost. Engraved into the modest stone, just above the hard flower heads, there was a single name, and below that an epitaph. She read both slowly, as though for the first time, though she was sure she had seen them a hundred times before and not remembered:

HERE LIES ROBERT RANKIN

"A MAN SEES IN THE WORLD
WHAT HE CARRIES IN HIS HEART"

She thought for a long time about the wording of the inscription. She supposed she had chosen it herself. She must have felt something, even then; a stirring of uneasiness at the idyllic village. Guilt might have played a part in its choice. She might just have liked the statement. Either way, it resonated now more than ever before.

Her eyes fell to the bouquet of flowers at the headstone's base. Frost had done terrible damage to them, but it still roused her to see something there. She wondered who might have brought them, who continued to replace them, year after year. Ms. Andrews had been responsible for this place once. Freya hoped that, faced with the question, she might have remembered if it was her. There was still much she could not recall, or ever would. She was almost free...

Many were the times George had stood before the headstone. Perhaps he had sensed something, the bond of blood between father and son; an ancestral connection, drawing him back to the grave when he passed it. Robert had passed on the hunger, as his father before him, and his father before that. It was not so hard to think an instinctual love coursed through the same blood.

She lingered a moment longer, then turned from the grave and left. It was all superfluous now. She visited the spot with the detached nostalgia of someone who has moved on. There was no other way for it. She didn't even know if there was anything left to bury after that night. The ritual of mourning was just that; another needless ceremony. So she said her goodbyes and walked from the churchyard for the last time.

* * *

A restlessness filled the empty village, as a clutch of insect eggs eager to hatch. She sensed that tonight was

Midwinter. Time and dates were reduced to night and day now, but the wind and trees and the empty houses spoke to her as she moved through them and they told her that tonight was the night when instincts raged and Lynnwood filled with howls.

When she arrived home Lizzie had gone. She could only imagine where the girl ran, now that she was freed. The village had driven Lizzie half to death, but in the end her hunger had saved her. The hunger, which was so normal in their insane world of rules and regulations, laws and limitations, schools and streets and manners...

The soft pink of fading afternoon crept into the sky, and she realised this was her last day as Freya. So much of her had gone already, lost the night she had chased Robert through the trees, then covered up; replaced with propriety and false smiles and a lifetime of habits designed to keep her satisfied. But there was no satisfying that hunger for life, no sating that appetite. It lived always, under her skin, growing stronger with each passing year.

She found herself food, which she ate ravenously. Seated at the dining table, she stared out of the window. The cottage opposite was still. Empty. Nothing stirred – there was no one left to stir, except hungry ghosts, and they would come soon enough. She knew she would forget soon. It did not seem to matter now that everyone was gone, and their mild manners, their modesty, with them. The village was full of these things before. To forget them would be bliss. She was so close to forgetting, and to the freedom forgetting brings.

But others might come, one day in the future. They

would come when the village was silent, its occupants missed. So she must write, before she forgets. She must write this for them. She had never written anything before, beyond schoolgirl diaries, and those seemed so long ago now.

* * *

She no longer remembers things, but lives them. She moves through the shadows of the undergrowth. Branches scratch her, each nick, each flare of pain real and sensuous. Her blood, so hot, cools rapidly against her skin. She can smell it, coppery and rich on the night air. She moves quickly through the Forest.

Her nose fills with other scents. This low to the ground, she can smell the soil, even beneath the layer of snow. It is earthy, regenerating. She smells the cold air, the frozen Forest, the salty sweat of other animals. They are invigorating aromas. They bear no traces of town life, the vagaries of village existence. This is home now. It always has been. She has returned to the dark beneath the trees, where all things hunt or are hunted.

She thinks of very little but the wind in her face and the pull of the moon, high above. It does not illuminate the Forest – there is no piercing that darkness! – but it glances from the branches, throwing them into black relief. She pushes through these thickets, past tall trunks, and slinks through the hollows of trees, faster, faster, her eyes wide and watering.

The Forest feels endless. She cannot see past the trees, only vaguely aware of other things; muddied water, frozen into a swathe of ice, the crunch of the snow beneath her hands and feet, spotted brown where she has bled. Her wild eyes scour the undergrowth. Her breath is ragged in her throat. Her fingers scrabble through the snow, grow numb and become red. The feeling that drives her seems to swell inside. It gnaws, growing desperate, pushing at her chest, turning her stomach with sickness. She might have had a name for this feeling once. Now it is beyond names. She knows it only as a part of her, pressing against her skin, filling her heart, her eyes, her mouth, until she collapses beneath a tree and it erupts from her, a singular shriek...

The sound fills the Forest, then is swallowed by it. She sinks to the base of the tree, where she lies amid snowdrops. Her hurried breathing becomes slow, shallow, as though stolen by the snow. Her bright eyes dim and something stirs in the depths of her mind. Memories of former times: shapes skipping through Forest paths, green wellies, laughter lighting up a child's face. Headstones, warm wine the colour of blood, the insect hum of the refrigerator. Muddy fur against her fingertips, a smiling man's face, the Forest, cut and stuck and pasted with poignancy against a blank piece of paper...

Another sound slips past her lips. Low and forlorn, it seems to last forever, before finally trailing off.

Then she hears something, which causes her head to rise, her eyes to widen, her breath to catch. An answering howl, off through the trees. It echoes into the night, followed moments later by a second. Her heart is racing now, as though clawing to escape her chest. She pushes from the tree and begins to run again.

The Forest slides past. She moves quickly through the

trees, looking but not seeing. Her senses are tuned elsewhere. She listens for the howls, which rise erratically into the night. Sometimes they sound nearer, other times further off. The cold air fills her nostrils and for one brief moment she loses herself completely to the Forest. It is transcendental. She feels the cold, sees the night, hears the trees and the pulsing of her blood in her head, and she is complete...

Two shadows slink from either side of her, running at her heels. They are smaller, thinner, but no less wild, filled with the ecstasy of the hunt. Together, mother and offspring race between the trees, hungry and alive.

Sparkling Books

Young adult fiction

Cheryl Bentley, *Petronella & The Trogot*
Brian Conaghan, *The Boy Who Made it Rain*
Luke Hollands, *Peregrine Harker and The Black Death*

Crime, mystery and thriller fiction

David Stuart Davies, *A Taste for Blood*
Nikki Dudley, *Ellipsis*
Sally Spedding, *Cold Remains*
Sally Spedding, *Malediction*

Other fiction

Anna Cuffaro, *Gatwick Bear and the Secret Plans*
Amanda Sington-Williams, *The Eloquence of Desire*

Non-fiction

Daniele Cuffaro, *American Myths in Post-9/11 Music*
David Kauders, *The Greatest Crash: How contradictory policies are sinking the global economy*

Revivals

Gustave Le Bon, *Psychology of Crowds*
Carlo Goldoni, *Il vero amico / The True Friend*

For more information visit:
www.sparklingbooks.com

Sparkling Books